Knights of the

Arrowhead

Jerry Terrebrood

Paperback-Press
an imprint of A & S Publishing
A & S Holmes, Inc.

ISBN-13: 978-1945669026
ISBN-10: 1945669020

ACKNOWLEDGMENTS

Several of my friends have previewed my manuscript, but two of them contributed significantly to the novel itself: **John Hamilton** recommended a chapter sequence change which was extremely constructive in the chronology of events. My nephew **Hank Terrebrood, Jr**. contributed history and focus to many areas of the book.

My thanks to these helpful contributors.

INTRODUCTION

Growing up, my favorite movies and publications were Westerns. Of course, as I aged, life taught me that the hero isn't always that heroic, the heroine isn't always that pure, things don't always work as planned, and sometimes in real life, the hero doesn't ride off into the sunset with the prettiest girl in town. So, in 1992, I began writing this—in my mind a more realistic kind of novel.

This Western begins with the lives of the main characters and youthful fantasies. It continues with: decisions in life and the consequences thereof; expectation often being greater than the realization; the hardening effects of life; and in the end; recognition of the more important values of life.

Jerry Terrebrood

CHAPTER 1

"Tucker Spence, you brat!   I hate you!" she screamed.

Tucker laughed as he ran, easily outdistancing the distressed young girl.

"Naw ya don't, Becky Ragine Hughes, ya know ya love me," he taunted over his shoulder.

"When I catch you, you... beast! I'll show you just how much I love you!"

"Tucker!   What did 'ya do t' that poor girl now?" his father called from the barn. "Looks t' me like you'd leave her be once in a while, she's only got two more days t' visit. You want her t' leave rememberin' you as the idiot neighbor boy? Come over here!"

Tucker ran to the barn where his father stood. He knew his father wasn't really mad at him. Nobody in the world was a bigger tease than his pa.

Ed Spence masked his face with sternness, but there was a betraying twinkle in his eyes. "Whad'ya do?"

"Poured a jar of tadpoles in her lap," Tuck answered gleefully.

Ed shook his head in mock consternation. "You kinda like her doncha?"

"Naah, she's jist a dumb ole girl, Pa!" The comment was aimed at Becky who had just that moment arrived at the barn door. Her face was bright red from exertion and anger.

Like a cat Tucker raced up the ladder to the hayloft. Becky scrambled after him, the front of her dress still soaked from his dousing. Upon reaching the loft, exhausted from her efforts, Becky collapsed in the hay.

Ed Spence moved on to his chores.

Tucker watched her from his hiding place. Her breathing was rapid and heavy. Her face was still flushed. His eyes were riveted on the rhythmic rise and fall of her budding puberty.

When at last she was able to breathe normally and her face began to cool, she sat up. "Alright, you no good thing... come out!" There was no anger left in her voice. In fact she sounded amused.

Tuck stayed where he was. He'd learned from girls in school that they couldn't be trusted. Just when you thought they'd quit they wouldn't. He remembered the time that all he had done was pick up a girl's pigtail that was swishing around on his desk. She'd only told him to quit once. Then she turned around, smiled sweetly, and stabbed him in the back of the hand with a writing quill. He still carried an ink spot in the back of his hand as a reminder.

"Come on out. I won't do anything. You're not afraid of a dumb old girl are you?" she said mockingly.

Tuck stayed put.

"Tucker Spence! I am going home if you don't quit hiding." Becky looked around the loft in frustration trying to spot him. A few moments passed with Tuck still observing from his hiding place. Becky picked up a piece of straw to examine it. "I wanted to say something to you before summer is over and I have to go back to Philadelphia."

Something in her voice gave Tuck a queer sensation. He wasn't sure just what it was.   All summer long he had looked for a chance to tell her how he really felt about her. Maybe she felt the same way about him and was about to tell him. Wouldn't that be something? Then, all he'd have to do would be just act really calm and mature and say something like, he'd thought some about her too.

He crawled out from his hiding place. "Whadda ya wanna say?" It could still be a trick. She might have something to throw. He watched her carefully.

She motioned for him to come over and sit by her. She had pulled her knees up under her chin and her dress was draped over them. She was turned toward him just enough for him to get a slight glimpse of a milky white thigh.

Tuck felt a strange tingling sensation and tightness in his throat. The tingling was sort of in his stomach but maybe down in his legs. He tried to take a step toward her. His legs didn't seem to want to move. He was feeling a little warm and queasy.

His throat felt like he'd swallowed a crab apple. There was something strangely magnetic about the way she was looking at him. Try as he might, he could not take his eyes away from the sight of her slightly exposed thigh. Tuck had never experienced anything like this before.

He wanted to sit beside her and yet feelings of caution and confusion made him wait.   He   was afraid to believe that this might be the moment he'd wished for all summer long.

"Please come over here and sit by me Tucker," she implored.

Boy, Tuck thought, *when you got really close to them you just felt a lot different than normal.* He'd had this problem before with girls at school but never this bad. He didn't understand it. Just about everything girls did was disgusting. But, when you got up real close to one, especially a pretty one, she didn't seem all that disgusting. Tucker was disgusted with himself however, for the way he was feeling. He felt like a fool. There just wasn't anything he could do to make the feelings stop.

Becky patted the straw next to her. "Come on. I won't bite you."

Somehow his feet found life. He stepped over and sat down in the straw next to her.

"Tucker, when I go home today I won't be back until next year. My Aunt Nell and Uncle Jake are taking me to see one of my cousins tomorrow and then I leave on the train from there. I was hoping we could have spent the day doing something besides you being a typical dumb boy, but now the day is almost over."

He wasn't sure he knew what she was referring to about him being dumb. There wasn't anything dumb about boys! However, this didn't seem to be the time to argue the point.

He was fearful she might notice he was sort of vibrating everywhere. The more he tried to suppress it the worse it got. He knew he wasn't cold, but he was shivering. She didn't seem to notice however, and he did his best to appear calm as she continued.

"Tucker, have you ever kissed a girl?"

Suddenly, there was a dropping sensation in his stomach. For several moments Tuck just looked at Becky. He had heard the question but his mouth wouldn't work. It was too dry. He felt a slight sensation of dizziness. It was good that he was already sitting down. His mind struggled to compose a response. While he hadn't actually kissed a girl, he had kissed his pillow while he thought about kissing a girl. *Oh Lord,* he thought, *don't let my mouth say anything that dumb!* In reply he could only shake his head no.

"Would you like to kiss me?" she asked, with the lips he'd been awake so many nights thinking about and yearning to experience.

Becky's eyes were large liquid pools of brown. She had soft golden hair. Her tiny nose was lightly sprinkled with freckles.

Tucker opened his mouth but nothing came out. He was really dry now. He sat sort of leaned over bracing himself on one hand, but now his elbow was quivering and threatening not to hold him up. He nodded in the affirmative.

"Then do it!" she said imperiously.

Tucker Spence was stone except for that vexing and incessant shiver throughout his body. He just sat and looked at her.

Suddenly she placed one hand behind his head and grasped his trembling elbow with the other. She kissed him forcefully and deliciously on the lips. Sounds disappeared and the hayloft spun. She held the kiss for what seemed to him a very long time. Tuck feared he was going to run out of breath, collapse, and fall over backward.

Finally, she relaxed and withdrew her lips from his. She brushed his cheek with another kiss and whispered, "You were right Tucker. I do love you."

His heart was pounding in his chest. His face was aflame with the thrill of the moment. His breathing was rapid as excitement ruled his body.

She stood and began to leave.

"Wait!" he heard himself finally manage to say.

Becky sat back down in the hay beside him. Tuck put his arm around her shoulders to pull her to him. As he did, Becky laid back into the fresh hay. He was now leaning over her with his face only inches from hers. He could see her nostrils flaring slightly with each breath she took. Her face was flushed again and her eyes were mysterious and inviting pools. Tucker pressed his lips against hers and she encircled his neck with her arm pulling him tightly to her.

When their lips parted, Becky whispered, "Touch me." Tuck was motionless, not knowing what she meant. She took his free hand and guided it to her breast. With her hand on top of his she squeezed his fingers into her flesh and he heard her moan quietly but in a way that made his senses reel.

Suddenly, she pushed him away and stood to her feet. There was a knowing smile on her face as she gazed at this young boy whom she had just escorted a small distance on his path toward manhood. She turned to go.

"Wait!" Tuck cried. He pushed his hand into his pocket and pulled out a small Indian arrowhead with a hole drilled in it. It had probably been a necklace ornament. It was Tuck's treasure. "Take this an' keep it forever. I love you Becky. Keep it with you and then you won't forget me. No matter where you go, or what happens, if ya ever need me send that to me. I'll know an' I'll come wherever ya are."

She took the tiny ornament and gazed at him without speaking. Her face was still flushed and her eyes were alive. She started to say something, checked herself, turned, and climbed down the ladder that led from the hayloft.

He watched from the loading door of the loft as she walked across the meadow to her Uncle's farm. In his mind he chastised himself. *Dumb! Dumb! Dumb! After all that happened, all you can think of to give her is an arrowhead. She won't keep it. It won't mean anything to her. You should have picked her a flower or something girls would like to keep.*

It was a moment to remember. But, it had all been nearly forgotten over time, because Becky never came to visit again.

CHAPTER 2

It was 1856. Rising tensions between the pro-slavery states and the abolitionists occupied much of the thought and conversation of the people in the Ozarks. Over the next two years, three groups, the Bushwhackers and Border Ruffians from Missouri and Jayhawkers from Kansas, would continue to engage in hostilities which would help to ignite the Civil War between the Northern Unionists and the Southern Secessionists.

Border Ruffians were pro-slavery activists who attempted to force the acceptance of slavery in Kansas. This group was probably best described as an armed gang of rag-tag, too-poor-to-own-a-slave racists, who were driven to action through the fear mongering of Missouri Senator David Rice Atchison. Atchison was openly supportive of violence; if in support of the slave owners' way of life. He once announced that *Missourians should kill every "damned abolitionist" in the district.*

In 1855 Atchison had led a Border Ruffian mob of more than five thousand into Kansas. There they used force of arms to take over polling places and cast tens of thousands of fraudulent pro-slavery candidate votes which resulted in a pro-slavery legislature for Kansas.

Border Ruffians twice sacked the town of Lawrence, Kansas. The second attack saw eight hundred Ruffians enter the small town and control all entry and egress. Buildings were destroyed or burned.

Bushwhackers were small groups of non-military men aligned with the slave states who operated in the bush using guerrilla warfare tactics. They were excellent marksmen and chose to pick off leaders and send Jayhawker troops into disarray. Adding to the problems of the already burdened battlefield, regular patrols had to be organized to locate these snipers–Rebel soldiers would employ these same Bushwhacker tactics throughout the Civil War.

The Jayhawkers, formed in the border state of Kansas, were generally thought of at home as abolitionists. In reality, the group was an organized band of privateers and professionals that wanted nothing more than to profit from the conflict. The group had a strong leader in a former US Senator by the name of James H. Lane. He and fellow Jayhawkers' movement leader, Charles "Doc" Jennison, a former member of the 7th Kansas Cavalry unit, would ride into the slave state of Missouri and kill white owners while setting slaves free.

One of the worst of the Jayhawker raids was executed in Missouri in 1861; the home state of Tucker Spence. The massacre at Osceola, Missouri saw the entire town of three thousand razed via vandalism and fire. The raiders went on to kill seventeen members of a small Southern force and finally executed nine of Osceola's citizens.

Growing up in these times, and knowing of these events, Tuck had developed a keen sense of not just right and wrong, but equality and justice. His sense of right and wrong pushed him out of alignment with many of his fellow Missourians.

When Tuck announced to his pa that he had decided to join the Union Army, His pa had a conversation with him:

"Tuck, yer headed into a situation that will require you to think like, act like, and be a man. Now these 'r a lot easier said than done son. A man has t' decide what he's gonna be and what he's not gonna be. A real man has t' stand fer doin' what's necessary every time, and doin' what's right all the time. Don't matter whether it's popular or convenient. Ya do it because it is necessary and it is right, regardless of what others may think or do. Now where do you stand on this slavery issue son? We don't own any slaves and do ya think it's really our business?"

Tuck's brow furrowed for a moment as he formed his reply:

"Pa, I don't think any man owns any other man, ner should hold another man or woman as a slave. If people work for ya, they should be paid a wage. I figure a man owns his own hands and he ought to be the one t' determine where they're gonna be used. You taught me that we're all God's children... I guess I'll stand by that. An' just cuz some folks can't fight back against things that's wrong, don't mean they should be abused. I reckon that's how I feel."

Ed Spence smiled at his man child and said to him, "Alright son, I agree with yer thinkin' so go do what ya need t' do." Inside his heart was nearly bursting with pride. He knew he had raised a young cub that had turned into a lion. "But, there's one more thing. In war, it's kill 'r be killed. Yer comin' off the farm and yer gonna run into some real hard cases out there. Lotta men ain't got no conscience when it comes to killin' somebody. Lot of 'em 'r just plain vile down t' the core. When the time comes in war, killin' the enemy is understandable. But there are other men who will be feedin' off the lives and blood of the soldiers, the widows, and the defenseless. They won't have one hesitation about killin' t' get what they want. That kind o' feller needs killin' himself. Can't be no hesitation Tuck, it's them 'r you. Make sure it's them. If ya don't get that stuck deep in yer noggin, you'll be comin' back t' me in a pine box."

By the time of the Osceola massacre in 1861, Tuck had already made his bed with the abolitionists and was a member of the Union Army.

Becky Hughes, would spend her teenage years in Philadelphia and escape the perils of the Civil War.

Despite being Southern sympathizers due to the commerce ties with the south, the second largest city in the United States quickly sided with the abolitionists. This fortuitous change of side sparked new commercial traffic in medical supplies, uniforms and shipbuilding for the Union Army.

The fighting never entered Philadelphia, thanks in part to the Washington Grays, a Light Infantry unit of the Pennsylvania Volunteers already fighting with the Union Army, the Philadelphia 20th Emergency Regiment, and the First City Troop. The two latter units participated in fighting and burning of the bridge which prevented Lee from crossing the Susquehanna River at Wrightsville; a stone's throw from Philadelphia.

Privilege and wealth had a telling effect on many naïve young women in those days. Women were sheltered from as many of the horrors of life as possible–It was this *naiveté* that would play a major role in the downfall of Becky Hughes.

Two years after the Civil War ended Becky met Mason Broome in Philadelphia through her father who had been boyhood friends with Mason's father. Mason had come to Philadelphia to attend a political conference, and, at her father's invitation, stayed with them for the duration.

Mason was blessed with rugged good looks, a keen sense of humor, great intellect, and a good education. He was already representing a large constituency in Kentucky at major political gatherings in the east. As her father had repeatedly pointed out to her, Mason Broome had substance and a bright future.

They were soon married and Becky found herself departing the train station at Broad and

Prime Streets heading toward Lexington, Kentucky known at the time as "Athens of the West".

CHAPTER 3

Becky sat staring out her window across the broad open expanse that surrounded the huge house. The same house that had held so much wonder and excitement for her when she first saw it was now her prison. Tears coursed down her cheeks as she pondered the events that had brought her to her present circumstances. How could she have been so blind, so stupid?

It had been a gorgeous Indian summer's day in Kentucky when Becky first met Klaus Vogel. He was a tall, blond, and athletic, German nobleman who had come to this country only months before to escape what he would describe only as "persecution" in his own country. To Becky, he was gallant, charming, and dazzlingly handsome. Becky was swept away by him at their first encounter.

The problem was that she was already married to Mason Broome whom she respected and admired tremendously. Although she wasn't sure she loved

Mason, she was sure she would learn to as time went by. He was the kind of man every girl set her cap for.

As the years passed, she was relatively satisfied with her decision. she was enamored with Kentucky and thrilled with their estate. It was graced with lush bluegrass, stately trees, bountiful crops, and majestic, spirited, horses. She thought herself content for many years until the arrival of Klaus.

Klaus was a distant relative of her husband's through the Broome's family members still living in Europe. Mason was immensely flattered when a letter arrived stating that Klaus was relocating to America and inquiring whether Mason could assist him in establishing a horse breeding enterprise. Mason's first love was horses.

Klaus and Mason got along exceptionally well. Klaus was a man of significant financial means and was interested in the purchase of only the finest stock and equipment. He shared Mason's own philosophy that blooded stock consumed no more feed than scrub horses and certainly rewarded the initial investment to a greater degree.

Becky was both thrilled and abashed by the intensity of her feelings when she was in the presence of Klaus Vogel. She realized as a married woman she had no right to give vent to, or even allow the initiation of, such feelings. She knew, but simply could not repress infatuation borne upon the fluttering wings of a foolish heart.

Klaus was acutely aware of the effect he had upon her. In private moments, he made her acutely aware he knew. She was like a moth circling ever closer to the flame. Becky was not, however, a senseless insect. She knew full well the consequences if she were found too near the fire. Nonetheless, it began with his knee touching hers under the table at a dinner with friends one warm summer evening. It began, and she had wanted it to.

She was convinced in her heart she would never purposely hurt Mason, but her desire for this bold and handsome man cried out to be satisfied if in only the smallest way. Desire for a fortuitous touch soon gave way to the creation of moments to be secretly together. Her desire became a driving force out of control and she was swept along by its torrent. She was fearful of discovery, but too enthralled by the clandestine moments to deny herself the pleasure of them.

When he held her and kissed her it was magic. He kissed her with a kind of force and emotion she'd never known with Mason.

She remembered being somewhat disappointed on her wedding night. She had expected much more; more emotion, more passion, more of a thrilling moment. She had accepted that perhaps she had maintained unrealistic expectations. She was obliging whenever Mason signaled his desire for her, but it was more of a submission to her husband and a willingness to please. But with Klaus, she felt an animalistic arousal in her that roared its desire to be released and clawed within her to be set free. It consumed her thoughts in the daytime and stalked her dreams at night.

But, the day finally came for Klaus to leave. Becky was both remorseful and glad. She knew she would ache for the romantic fulfillment only his presence could bring. She was also very relieved she had not been found out. She vowed she would never again allow herself to be involved in such a potentially devastating situation with anyone ever again. It was autumn when Klaus departed.

Winter was long and dragged by uneventfully. She often found herself lost in daydreams of Klaus. Her nights were restless and for the first time she began to resent Mason's uninspired attempts at lovemaking.

When spring finally arrived, Mason sallied forth to ply the craft of politics in the east. She had begged Mason to take her with him, but he would not. Becky found herself alone and empty at a time when the entire world was being refreshed and renewed.

She struggled to erase the memories of Klaus thinking that time, the great healer, would scar over the empty void in her soul.

Mason had been in the east for more than a month when she received his letter stating the first really beneficial legislation was in process and he owed it to his constituents and their future to ensure Kentucky was represented in every facet of the proceedings. He apologized but was certain in midsummer he could return.

She sat in the orchard for most of that day under the flowering trees too depressed to savor the perfume of their blossoms. She clutched the letter and grieved for herself. It wasn't that she missed Mason so much as it was a feeling of despair from wasting away uselessly alone. She was not good at being alone.

One day, on a bright spring morning, a carriage drove up the lane of her estate and stopped in front of the house.

A servant had announced the approaching carriage and Becky had watched from a drawing room window as the horses trotted briskly toward the house. She wondered who it could be. She certainly wasn't expecting anyone. Then she saw him. It was Klaus. Her heart pounded and she felt needles of excitement all over her body. He looked more marvelous than she remembered. The urge to run to him was nearly irresistible

As he ascended the steps of the great porch she could wait no more. She flung the door wide and ran to take his hands. "Klaus! Whatever are you doing here? Mason is gone... he's away on business."

"I know," was his reply. Klaus held her hands tightly and smiled handsomely. He ushered her into the house and closed the door behind him. Looking around to ensure they were alone, he kissed her passionately and fully upon the lips. Her knees weakened and she thought her heart would beat her into unconsciousness.

When he finally released her she protested dutifully, if feebly. In truth she was thrilled. "Klaus, you can't... we can't... this can't happen again."

"Ssh! Bekk, I haf come for you."

"What? What are you talking about?"

"You know vut I'm talking about, mein Bekk... for you I haf come... you vanted me to... you know it... I know it... I am here." His English was rather fluent. The trace of German accent had a cultured flair unlike the gutturalness of many Germans unaccustomed to the English language. To Becky his accent had a charming lilt that made everything he said musical and precious. His voice was soft and crooning as he whispered endearments while holding her pressed firmly against him.

"I... I can't," she murmured.

"You must."

"How... how can I?"

"I haf everything arranged. I haf everything you vill need. Come vith me now. I can give you the life you have always dreamed of."

"Oh, Klaus... I... I have to think... I can't just walk out of here... you don't understand... I have things... I have a husband... you can't just expect me to–" He kissed her again deeply and passionately. Fires ignited within her and reason began to fail.

As the day continued, there were moments where reason began to prevail. She found herself reconsidering. This was no schoolgirl crush to be blindly followed. After all, she was leaving her husband, her family, and all of the things that made for a stable life to run away with a man who was taking her to a place she knew nothing about to live in a style she knew nothing about. Where was her mind?

But, Klaus was masterful at persuasion and each time she raised an objection his response, his touch and his kiss, persuaded her that all would be wonderful. He described his ranch to her in great and glowing detail. His description included every aspect of the home he'd established, the scenic beauty of the surroundings, and the great herd of horses his money had amassed. He made it all sound so heavenly. It would be the kind of life she'd had in Kentucky as well as the fulfillment of her passion, which with Mason she had never known.

By afternoon his urgings had countered all of her protests. She packed as many of her indispensable personal things as she could and left with him. As she exited the door, she thought of leaving Mason a letter, but then, what could she say that wouldn't be more painful than if he just found her gone?

The first few days were marvelous passionate bliss. She had been swept away on a swift carriage ride to Lexington where they would leave on the railway early the next morning. .

They left on the Louisville, Cincinnati and Lexington railway at 6:15 a.m. and arrived in Louisville at 10:45 a.m. It was a four and a half hour ride west to the banks of the Ohio River. After disembarking from the train, it was time for lunch. Since the Ohio and Mississippi train to St. Louis didn't depart until 7 p.m., a shopping excursion followed by dinner was in order. Over dinner and a sip of Kentucky bourbon, they remarked what a shame it was there hadn't been an event at the Jockey Club and Driving Park Association grounds that afternoon; they might have enjoyed Kentucky's two famous attributes in a single day.

The Kentucky Derby was only three years old but William Clark's grandson, Meriwether, had leased the 80 acres from Henry Churchill. His efforts were successful at introducing horse racing in the style of the English Derby and Epsom Downs.

That evening, the Ohio and Mississippi line carried them across the Ohio River and westward toward St. Louis. The overnight trip gave them time to enjoy each other's company in a private room on a sleeper car. It was as romantic and exciting to her as any fantasy she had ever had.

St. Louis would be their host for the greater part of the day after their 7:10 a.m. arrival. It was here she thought back to her childhood and Tucker Spence for the first time in many years. The sweetness of the memory was fleeting and her mind soon returned to the events of the current moment.

After dinner and a stroll to the Atchison and Nebraska line for a scheduled 9:07 p.m. departure, they were once again on their way west.

As the sun rose the next morning, Becky watched from the window as their westward trip traversed the marvelous open country. She was hoping to perhaps see a remaining buffalo. She had recently read their numbers were dwindling in the face of a government supported cull. The newspaper article explained this had been designed to wipe out the major food source for the Indians, forcing them on to government reserves and thus making the frontier safer for travel.

At 2 p.m. that afternoon they made a hasty change for the newly restructured St. Joseph and Western at Troy Junction. From there they traveled on to Kearney and at nine fifteen that evening changed for the Union Pacific to Cheyenne. They were to arrive at 1:20 in the afternoon on the following day.

As the train pulled into the station she reflected on the romance of the trip and the delicious company of this handsome German whose commanding presence continued to sweep her along with abandon.

It was an intoxicating adventure; made more exciting by her imaginations of the promise of her new life with this man she loved.

Her conscience did occasionally nag her. Each time however, the foolishness of her heart and the fire of her desire ignored her inner part that cried caution.

When the train finally arrived in Cheyenne, the ranch foreman met them. He was a small swarthy man and Becky was extremely uncomfortable around him. However, it became immediately apparent he was careful not to incur the displeasure of Klaus, so Becky dismissed her fears.

The trip by carriage to the ranch was wonderful. Fresh outdoor air scented with the fragrance of countless wild flowers and grass. Her eyes drank in the wonder of the vast, almost treeless, prairie blanketed with a sea of buffalo grass. They crossed a creek. Cottonwood and willow trees grew in profusion on its banks. Occasionally she glimpsed some form of wild life. Klaus assured her that animals roamed freely and abundantly.

Still, there was an occasional trace of remorse over her capricious act. She tried hard not to consider its inevitable devastating impact upon all who knew and loved her. She fought back tears as she reflected upon what her father would think. It was too late now though. She was committed to Klaus and to love. That's all that really mattered. This was her opportunity for real happiness and she had seized it.

After three days of travel through the open country and nights camped out in the open, the sight of the big house sitting in the middle of a large open expanse of grassland with corrals and outbuildings a great distance away was very impressive. There was a fence completely around the huge lot dedicated to the house. A large gate in the fence crossed the rutted drive leading to the front door.

At the gate the foreman stepped down from his horse and opened it. Klaus drove her to the door of her new home.

Without a word Klaus swept her from the carriage in his arms and carried her through the large double doors of the house.

That night she experienced Klaus's passion in a fullness she had not yet known with him. As she drifted off to sleep she was reassured in her heart that whatever price she had paid to be with him, the rewards were surely greater than the price paid.

The next morning was her first realization that the price had not been fully paid.

CHAPTER 4

Klaus was up before dawn and when Becky opened her eyes to admire her new lover he spoke curtly to her.

"Get up. You vill start my breakfast. After vich, you vill clean house und mek sure you haf dinner ready for me at midday. I haf vork that must be done. So... get up."

Becky sat up and looked at him questioningly. She thought that he was joking and laughingly replied, "Yes, master."

Klaus stared at her coldly and walked to the side of the bed. He reached out and grabbed her by the front of her nightdress and yanked her from the bed on to her feet.

"Yes, I am your master. Soon you vill know just vut that means. Now do as I haf instructed und do it now."

Becky could not believe what she was hearing. She was shocked by the manner in which she had been yanked from the bed. He was not joking.

The realization flooded in upon her in a wave of fear, revulsion, and anger. She turned him around to face her as he began to leave.

"What do you think this is? Who do you think you are? I don't have a master! If you think I came all this way to be treated like this you think again! I'll thank you to arrange my return today!"

Klaus slapped her hard across the face.

Her knees buckled as the sound and the pain of the slap exploded in her head. Darkness rushed in momentarily and she felt herself falling across the bed.

He slapped me! My God! He actually slapped me! Her mind was screaming but shock had stricken her momentarily dumb. Her senses reeled at the pain of the burning welts on her face and the throbbing ache in her head.

Before she could regain her composure he picked her up by the front of her nightdress again and held her in such a way that only her toes still touched the floor.

"Now! You vill go down und cook for me... just as I haf said."

The words came from a face twisted with cruelty. She could see in his eyes a fierce and fiendish glint and she knew that Klaus was experiencing sick pleasure from his actions. She was powerless against him and that was exactly what he was demonstrating to her.

"Damn you! You bastard!" she spat.

Something exploded in her head and darkness swept over her.

When she awoke, her face was throbbing and her left eye ached. It would not open. She dragged herself from the bed over to a mirrored dresser. She staggered back in shock as the mirror revealed the raised welts on her face. Her eye, already swollen closed, was beginning to discolor as the blood pooled beneath the skin.

She rushed to the door with murder in her heart. No one could treat her like this! It was locked. "Oh my God! Oh my God! This can't be happening!" she screamed.

Shock had robbed her legs of strength and she barely managed to arrive at the bed when blackness swept her away again.

That was how long ago now? At first she held out hope that Mason would come and find her, but after many months, she had given up on the idea. Why should he come after a faithless wife?

The question came to her again, and again, and again, and still she had no answer: How could she have been so blind and so stupid?

During the course of the past years Becky had suffered so many cruel indignities at the hands of Klaus that she was not sure she was really in her right mind anymore. Sometimes it seemed like she was someone else watching all of this take place with a woman who looked and sounded like her but couldn't really be her. No, she was the wife of a gentleman of Kentucky horses and politics. This poor woman was an unfortunate soul who had the bad luck of belonging to a monster. One thing she was certain of. If she refused to speak at all it seemed better for that poor woman. She didn't really understand why that was, except that whenever she had said anything in the early months that poor woman, whoever she was, suffered horrible abuse because of it. It was Becky's responsibility to help the poor thing. So, if silence helped her case, Becky would remain silent. She wasn't sure who the poor unfortunate was, but she knew silence and obedience made things better.

The door flew open suddenly and Klaus stood in the opening. Becky flinched at the sound and the sight.

"Come!" As Klaus turned and walked away, a small, naked, and dejected figure followed in silence.

Klaus led her down the hall toward a room filled with voices and reeking of tobacco smoke. When Becky entered the room a hush fell upon the men gathered there. Klaus ordered her onto the bed in the center of the room. Silently, she obeyed.

It was Fall of 1880 when Mason Broome received a letter from one of the servants at his home in Kentucky. A week later Tucker Spence received a letter from Mason Broome.

CHAPTER 5

There was no sheriff or any other form of local government in Crayt. Folks just lived together. It wasn't much of a town and didn't have a lot of reasons for existence. There was a freight office, but it was only open one day each week to deliver and receive wagon freight to and from the railroad in Cheyenne. The post office was located in the town's only store where Bert, the proprietor, sold as wide a variety of items as the local traffic would support. There was of course a saloon. The rest of Crayt consisted of only a few houses surrounding the combination church and schoolhouse.

A creek ran a few hundred yards south of town. Its banks were lined with willows creating a long winding ribbon of green across the open expanse of dry grassland that surrounded the little island of civilization. Each day in Crayt was pretty much a repeat of the day before.

Today was sweltering. The afternoon sun beat

without mercy through the front door and windows of the saloon. Its unrelenting rays steadily intensified the heat inside. For the next few hours the interior of the saloon would be like an oven.

The hot afternoon air in the saloon became thick and musty from years of dust collecting in the rafters and the cracks of the board floor. The acrid odor of tobacco smoke and the putrid essence of stale beer, from countless spills, were sharply enhanced by the stifling heat.

Jack, the bartender, leaned against the bar attempting to avoid the hostile penetrating streams of the sun as they knifed their way through windows fogged by dust on the outside and yellowed by smoke on the inside. He stared vacantly out the door occasionally mopping his face with a towel.

Two old ranchers, Ned and Pete, sat playing cards.

"Ya know, if whoever it was that built this place would o' put the door on one o' the sides instead o' the front it wouldn't git so dad blamed hot in here," Ned complained. Pete, Ned's customary companion, grinned behind his cards as he sat with his chair tipped back against the wall. Ned always got hotter when he didn't have a good hand to play.

The bartender was still leaned up against the bar. His white shirt was drenched with sweat and it clung to his torso in several places. Without a break in his purposeless stare, he commented dryly, "Well, if the horses that wore the road in the dirt had been travelin' alongside the buildin' instead of the front, the door would prob'ly be on the side...

then you'd gripe about where they put the road."

Pete chuckled. He knew Ned seldom listened to anything said in return to him. Ned only cared that folks knew how he felt. It didn't seem too important to him what anyone else thought. Ned really didn't want or expect a reply from anyone. That was Ned's nature and it was reflected in the way he'd run his ranch for years. Ned said it and others did it. Until the aging Ned began gradually turning the ranching responsibilities over to his sons and began coming to town regularly, there hadn't been much for him to listen to. He wasn't used to it yet.

"Good one Jake" Pete responded. "Wasted–but good."

Two riders, now visible only as distant specks, were slowly closing the gap between themselves and Crayt.

The afternoon finally passed and the sun had fallen behind the storefront across the street. The two riders stepped down from their mounts tying them and the packhorses to the rail in front of the saloon.

At first glance, these men didn't appear to be much different than most of the men who lived in and around Crayt. One was tall and lean. His black hair was streaked with gray and his complexion was dark. His expression seemed to suggest a mild boredom with his surroundings. But, his eyes were alive and a closer observation would reveal he was keenly aware of those things around him. The other man was not as tall, but was thick and muscular. His complexion was fair in sharp contrast to the dark features of the man with whom he rode and his hair was the color of straw. His demeanor was far more intense than that of his friend. The shirts on both men were soaked through with sweat and caked with dust. They tied their holsters down before entering the saloon.

As they entered, Jack greeted them cordially.

"Where you fellas comin' from? An' what brings ya t' Crayt, if ya don't mind my askin'?"

The taller man laughed loudly. The laughter came in surprising contradiction to his outward appearance of apathy.

"Why, we heard all about yer dancin' girls an' sportin' houses. We rode hard fer seven days t' git here! Ain't that so Tuck?"

The man he addressed as Tuck had removed his hat to wipe the sweat band. He answered plainly, "If you say so."

Jack wiped the bar in front of them and continued, "Well it's plain t' see you fellas got lied to by somebody. Closest we come t' sportin' ladies is the freight road leadin' t' Cheyenne. What're you two drinkin?"

Both ordered whiskey and a beer chaser.

As the sun continued to set, dark clouds began to form over the great open expanse west of Crayt and lightning flashed over the distant horizon. The conversation between the ranchers and the bartender turned to speculation on the chances of rain. Ned claimed it was only heat lightning. Jack was convinced that it would rain before morning. Pete abstained.

The two travelers talked quietly to each other as they nursed their drinks at the bar.

As the hours passed the air began to cool, but it was heavy with humidity making the atmosphere inside the saloon feel even thicker.

Jim Link, the taller of the two strangers, asked if there were accommodations for men and horses that could be rented for the night. The bartender laughed.

"Fellas, this ain't no real town...Now Bert, he owns the store an' a horse barn behind. Ya might find some dancin' chickens an' sportin' dogs down there, but that's about all." He laughed as he slapped the bar rag on the bar and wiped it vigorously, greatly amused at himself.

The two strangers left the saloon and walked across the hard packed street to the store.

Bert, the store's proprietor, agreed to board their horses for a fee and told the men they could spend the night with their horses at no charge. Other than that, it was possible that Effie Parsons the schoolmarm might rent them a room. She had a big house and lived by herself. Bert recommended the barn. He had been in Effie's house, not far in, but far enough.

They took Bert's advice.

Back in the saloon, the two rancher's conversation had turned to a discussion concerning the strangers.

Ned asked Pete, "Reckon they're lookin' fer work?"

"Nope, them ain't cowhands."

"What makes ya think not?" Ned asked.

"I don't think not, I know not. Them two ain't teamed up t' chase cows together."

"Whadda ya mean?" Ned snorted.

Pete shook his head, peered over his cards, and gave Ned a condescending smile.

"Ned, ya jist ain't seen much o' the world have ya? Now me, I used t' work cattle down in Texas afore I came up here twenty year ago. An' I ain't fergot things I knowed afore I came."

Pete examined his cards intently without going further. Ned sat, looking at Pete expectantly, waiting for him to continue. When it became obvious that Pete had no intentions of continuing, Ned's exasperation took over.

"Oh well, 'scuse me Tex! Didn't know I was seated with a genuine Texas fortune teller. But, course now that I do, I'll listen real close so I can start t' be smart like you, instead o' bein' some dumb butt that's only raised thousands o' beeves, fed a wife and three boys, sometimes as high as fifteen hands, an' bred some o' the best stock in these parts. But then o' course, that ain't nothin' compared t' bein' a genuine Texas fortune teller."

Pete was thoroughly enjoying the moment. Ned was so easy to get started. He liked the way Ned got all red in the face and picked up speed and volume as he fumed. Pete did wish there was a little more challenge to it, but nonetheless, he never failed to enjoy it.

Ned was, as he claimed, a successful rancher. However, he was predictable and blunt and easy to rile when challenged on any point. Because he had accumulated considerable wealth, Ned was convinced he was the sole authority on most matters

Pete's ranch wasn't as big or as prosperous as

Ned's, but he'd done sufficiently well to provide his sons with more than he'd been provided with when he was a boy. And one thing Pete was absolutely sure of was that although Ned had more money, Pete himself was a whole lot smarter. That's just all there was to that.

After sufficiently savoring the moment, Pete began again.

"If you'da been watchin', you'da seen there was never a time when they wasn't checkin' the door. One 'r th' other, sometimes both, was always checkin' the door. Nuther thing is, they ain't rubbed enough fer cowhands. Ain't got no tears 'r patches in their clothes, no busted knuckle, 'r black fingernail, ner cuts on their hands. I don't mean they ain't capable o' rough work, jus' that they ain't been doin' any. Two things I learned t' identify early in my days in Texas: a gambler an' a gun handler. I don't think them boys is gamblers."

Ned finished his drink and sat his glass down hard

"Well, that's what we need up here, couple bandits runnin' round."

"Lordy Ned, I didn't say they wuz bandits! You prob'ly ain't seen no bandits neither. In the first place it'd be rare t' see bandits come in to a place an' not try t' make everybody know there was some bad men in the place. Most o' the ones I seen did anyway. They git some kinda sick satisfaction outa makin' everbody jumpy and scairt."

Ned held his hand up, signaling a brief halt, to interpose in his own defense.

"Well now Pete, we've had t' hang a few

rustlers up here!"

"I ain't talkin' 'bout rustlers!" Pete exclaimed, "They'd jist's soon sneak in an' sneak off without bein' seen." He paused to take a drink of the beer he'd been nursing for the past hour before he continued.

"Nope, I'm talkin' about the kind that ain't happy unless they're bein' seen an' noticed. Sorta makes 'em keep doin' it. Usually ain't no sense t' kill another man over what they kill people for. They just have t' do it t' keep up with whatever their sick need is." Pete paused again to light the smoke he had rolled from his makings.

"I ain't talkin' 'bout them needin' food ner money. Most of 'em would kill ya fer that too. What they need most, only seems t' come when they get up over somebody else. Don't seem t' matter who it is, young'ns, women, farmers, cowhands, as long as they can make somebody scairt of 'em they're happy."

"Now those two, they don't seem t' care what you think of 'em and they have a kind of humble confidence, and a nearly polite way of bein'. They ain't normal gun handlin' ruffians and my bet is, it is best to not be on those boys' bad side."

Ned was leaned back in his chair having fairly well ceased to listen when it became plain that Pete was claiming to know more about a subject than Ned did. Noting that Pete had finally ended his philosophical discourse, Ned hastened to end the evening.

"Ya know what I think? I think yer fulla horse poop! An' I gotta git. See ya tomorrow."

Ned rose and left the bar.

CHAPTER 6

When morning broke rain was imminent. The sky was dark with heavy black clouds and thunder rumbled ominously. Lightning cracked close at hand producing a ringing sensation in Tucker Spence's ears as he stood gazing out the barn door. He needed a hot cup of coffee, a shave, and a bath.

Jim Link was propped up on his elbows seriously considering lying back down for a few more minutes of sleep in the first semblance of a bed they'd known since leaving Wichita. Bedding down in relatively fresh straw with a slab roof overhead might not have been hotel accommodations, but it was far better than sleeping out in the open, especially when it was going to rain.

"You gonna git up?" Tuck asked.

"Did ya ask 'em t' have the maid bring our breakfast yet?" Jim asked stretching and yawning. "You an' me don't exactly smell like lilies. I bet that's why the maid ain't in here yet. She took one whiff an' decided anything smelt that bad was prob'ly a long time dead. Course, it mighta been what kept the wolves away... Not a bear though. Bear would've ate us. He don't care what ya smell like."

"Git up," Tuck replied. "Might find breakfast an' a place t' clean up b'fore it cuts loose out here." Having given the invitation, Tuck walked out the barn door and up the gradual incline toward the front of the store.

Bert was a widower and lived in two rooms at the back of his store. He readily agreed to the provision of breakfast and the use of a washtub hanging on the back of the building. Bert wryly informed Tuck that if he hadn't asked about the tub he would have been sure to offer.

Bert raised a few chickens out back and had an ample supply of fresh eggs. To Tuck and Jim the thought of fresh eggs after many days on the trail was heaven.

The two men watched as Bert sliced thick slabs of smoked bacon and placed them in a hot black iron skillet. As the bacon fried, little curls of smoke rose above the stove from tiny spatters of grease that danced out of the pan on to the hot stovetop. The sizzle and the aroma of the frying bacon tantalized their senses. Bert poured them each a steaming cup of freshly brewed coffee.

After breakfast they set about the task of carrying water to the barn to fill the tub.

"You 'r me?" Tuck asked.

"I'll shave an' let ya warm the tub water up,"

Jim replied.

When the pair returned to the store Bert greeted them with a wide grin of approval suggesting they keep the tub to wash their dirty clothes in if they cared to. He obviously considered it his continuing civic duty to keep Crayt clean.

"You ever hear of a rich Dutchman that's got a big ranch near here?" Jim asked.

"You must be talkin' about Klaus Vogel. That's the only rich foreigner around here, only he ain't Dutch, he's German. There's a few German folk settlin' out here, but he's the only one I know of ya could call rich."

"I thought Vogel was a Dutch name," Jim replied.

"Nope, it ain't. It's German," Bert responded.

"Well, that's the right name," Tuck stated. "Ole Jim here fancies hisself a man of travels. Figgers he knows a lot about foreigners, Indians, and women." Tuck was gazing out the window and across the street at Jack who was unlocking the outer doors of the saloon.

"Why, thank ya Tucker, and ya might add that I am seldom wrong on any account," Jim said proudly.

"I might, if I hadn't jist heard ya be, an' if I hadn't seen that woman down t' Fort Worth nearly knock ya on yer backside. As I recall, I had to intervene with her brother who didn't care how drunk ya was. Ya do a might better with Indians though, I will admit t' that."

Jim burst forth with laughter. He had the laugh of a man who enjoyed something to laugh at. "Dang it Tuck, yer gonna totally ruin the mystery about me. An' that's what makes them women want t' jump on me in the dark."

"That's the only way you git 'em t' jump on ya is in the dark. If they see what they're gittin they're likely t' pass you by."

Jim shook his head and laughed again. "Bert, I'm quittin' while I still have some shred o' dignity left."

"You fellas thinkin' of goin' out to the Vogel place for a job? We don't know much about him... he ain't real sociable. Reckon it's 'cause of his accent, him bein' foreign an all. When him and his misses come in, he don't say much, an' I don't even know if she can talk American yet, or maybe can't talk at all. Nobody I know of has ever heard her utter a word. He does all the buyin' an' all the talkin'."

Tuck responded, "Is that right?" Without waiting for a reply, he and Jim left the store and walked across the street to the saloon.

"Mornin' fellas," Jack greeted them. "Its a little early... I was just lettin' in some cool air and sweepin' up, but I can stop and getcha whatever ya want."

"Ya think one o' them ranchers that was in here last night knows the *German* named Vogel?" Jim asked, placing significant emphasis on the word German for Tuck's benefit. "We hear he's got some o' the best horses in the territory."

"If you heard that, you heard more than I ever did. I don't know anything about him or his ranch. Pete prob'ly does if anybody does. Pete's pretty much aware of more than Ned is. Ned don't care too much about anything that ain't gonna line his pockets." Jack laughed at his own assessment of Ned and continued sweeping vigorously at something apparently stuck to the floor. Without looking up from his task, he told them that both men met shortly after noon every day except Sunday. When Jack finally did look up from his diligence Tuck and Jim were crossing the street headed back to the store.

Back in the barn they took Bert's suggestion and tended to their laundry needs hanging the wet garments on a rope stretched between two of the upright support posts.

"What next?" Jim asked.

"I figger we'll wait an' talk t' the ranchers. Maybe one o' them knows somethin' we need t' know b'fore we jist go ridin' out there."

"Wake me up when it's time," Jim said as he stretched out in the same straw he'd been so reluctant to leave that morning.

Tuck stood looking out the barn door, lost in thought, as large drops of rain began to fall. Small craters in the dust marked each drop that fell.

When the sun was at its highest, barely visible through the darkened sky, he awakened Jim and they headed for the saloon.

CHAPTER 7

Pete and Ned were seated at a table in the saloon sipping their first glass. A deck of cards lay in the middle of the table. The daily game had not yet begun.

"Mind if we sit?   Like t' ask a couple o' questions if ya don't mind." Without waiting for a reply to his question Jim pulled a chair back from the table and sat down. Tuck was still standing as the invitations to sit were being spoken. After they were extended he sat in the remaining seat.

"Questions are kinda like barter goods," Old Pete ventured, "if ya git t' ask 'em ya kinda lay yerselves open t' bein' asked some. How 'bout that?"

Pete's head was tilted slightly back and cocked a little to one side. He was peering at Tuck with obvious devilment in his tone and expression.

"Barter goods is based upon one thing bein' worth purty near t' what the other thing is," Tuck replied with his arms folded across his chest as he returned Pete's gaze.

"Well then, this ain't gonna be no fair deal a'tall! Me 'n Ned 'r old an' full o' interestin' stuff. You two prob'ly ain't packin' nowhere near as valu'ble stuff as we are."

Pete paused to grind out a cigarette butt, squinting his eyes against the smoke that curled up from the ashtray adding comic emphasis to the wry grin on his face.

"But, since yer young we might humor you some, jes so's you kin kinda git better prepared fer all o' the rough stuff we've been through. Right Ned?"

Ned looked at Pete blankly and made no reply.

"We hear there's a foreigner here that runs a real good string o' horses," Jim said, appreciative of Pete's humor, but pressing to get down to business.

"Vogel." Ned replied disdainfully. "He's got good horses an' cattle, but, I don't see how, he ain't got good sense."

Ned's comment was an opening that Pete could not resist. "Well hell Ned, you've got pretty good horses an' cattle too." he jibed.

Ned, failing to realize the inference, replied with genuine conviction, "You bet I do! I know what I'm doin'!"

Pete laughed aloud wagging his head in disbelief. "Well you fellas still got a question comin', cuz you tellin' us what ya heard ain't really a question. Course Ned's already give up a' answer fer free, but we're here t' help if we can." Pete said, still laughing, half at the fun of an interesting exchange with strangers, and half at Ned, who never seemed to be fully aware of the parts of any conversation that weren't coming directly from him.

"How many horses an' cattle does he run an' how many hands work for him?" Tuck asked.

"Why? You boys lookin' fer work?" Pete asked purposefully, remembering his conversation with Ned the previous night. He was anxious to establish his credentials as a credible discerner.

Jim wagged his index finger in mock admonition. "Oh no ya don't. We might be young, but we know enough t' realize that the answer to a question ain't another question."

Pete scrutinized Jim for a moment with new appreciation. For Pete, conversation was a skill and an art. Anyone could state facts, ask questions, and give answers. You had to be a cut above to make the process interesting.

Ned spoke first. "Well, Pete'll have t' tell ya all about Vogel, cuz I don't know. His place ain't close t' mine an' the only times I've seen 'im is here in town. He's 'n uppity jackass. Only time he'll speak is if he's buyin' sumthin' I reckon. Bert says he can talk American fair, but, if ya see 'im on the street 'r in the store he don't even return greetins. I don't like 'im an' sure ain't got no reason t' visit his place. You better ask the Texas fortune teller here." With that Ned got up and walked to the bar to inquire if Jack had made coffee yet.

"He's got about a hundred horses an' mebbe twice that in cattle I reckon," Pete supplied. "I spect in his best times he's got eight t' ten hands. I don't think he jist makes his livin' off a horses an' cattle though. He lives a way higher than his livestock'd bring him."

"How's that?" Jim asked.

Pete waved his finger in the same admonishing manner that Jim had displayed earlier. "Now actually you fellers 'r two questions up on us. One about stock an' one about cowhands."

Tuck grinned at the humorous old sage. "What would ya like t' ask that ya think we might know... us bein' young an' all?"

Pete was never one to rush the moment. He scooted his chair back from the table and leaned the back against the wall with his beer mug in his hand. He took a long swallow and then wiped both sides of his moustache with the back of his hand. "I o' course, bein' at the age o' consider'ble years of experience, an' not havin' lived a sheltered life like Ned has, already know the answer t' my question. But, for the sake o' my reputation as a 'genuine Texas fortune teller', I need t' have you boys bolster up my image some with Ned here."

Ned was returning with empty cups and a coffee pot. "What's that about Ned?" he asked as he reseated himself.

"Ask yer question," Jim said, enjoying the amusing exchange.

"Ned thinks some pretty strange things once in awhile... Hell, mebbe all the while. I don't know." Pete stopped to eye Ned quizzically for some rise from Ned or some visible effect but, as usual, the comment went unnoticed. "He gets these strange ideas like me bein' full of horse poop cuz I told him you two ain't cowhands. Now it's up t' you.

Remember, my reputation is ridin' on this, so think what yer mommas told ya 'bout the Bible sayin' that all liars 'r fryers... You boys ain't cowhands are ya?"

"Does yer question mean now 'r ever?" Jim asked.

"Now, and fer quite a while now."

"It's been sometime back since we chased cows fer a livin', maybe 'bout ten 'r more years an' it was our first an' last time if we kin help it. Ain't that right Tuck?"

With a wide grin Tuck challenged, "If we ain't cowhands what are we?"

"Ever been in Texas?" Pete asked, directing the question to Tuck.

"Been there, but we ain't from there."

"You boys remind me o' the fellers in Texas that makes their livin' with pistols and rifles," Pete stated with a touch of certainty.

Tuck decided to steer the conversation in another direction.

"Well, we ain't cowhands like ya said, but we ain't outlaws neither. We're out here t' buy brood stock fer a horse rancher. We don't herd 'em, jist look 'em over an' buy 'em. He pays t' have 'em delivered. That's why we wondered how many horses an' how many hands the German has t' drive 'em."

Pete's head was tilted back slightly and cocked to the side again in what was obviously his analytical position.

"Uh-huh, Well okay, if that's gonna be yer story." He knew when an issue was being skirted. "Tell ya what though. This's Saturday. Cowhands from the ranches 'round here'll be comin' t' town from 'bout suppertime t' however long it takes t' git in here from the ranch. I reckon some o' Vogel's hands'll be in here sometime. Ya might wanna ask them. They'll know all about his stock an' how many's workin' out there now. They kin prob'ly tell ya when's the best time t' talk to 'im. He ain't always sociable t' visitors they say."

"Jist might do that. Been a pleasure talkin' to a 'genuine Texas fortune teller' t'day. S'pose if me 'n Jim need a little more education you'd be available?" Tuck asked in jest.

Pete rolled another cigarette, licked the paper and smoothed the down the seal. He checked it over admiringly. "Well I'm mighty careful 'bout not wastin' m'self on useless work. However, you two do seem t' be a little better'n most o' the material I run across t' work with 'round here." He lit the cigarette, took a deep draw, and blew a cloud of blue smoke. "Course, I reckon yer both purty neart forty, that'll count some in yer favor. Any younger'n that an' the well o' my wisdom'd be a way over yer heads... sorta overwhelms the young an' the feeble."

Tuck and Jim were both laughing as they stood to leave.

Jim patted Pete's shoulder and then said to Tuck as they walked away, "Don't know how much that old boy knows, but he sure makes ya 'preciate the chance t' git it, don't he?"

CHAPTER 8

That evening, as Tuck and Jim returned to the saloon, the noise coming from inside greeted them while they were yet across the street.

"My, my, my... it do change on Saturday night," Jim observed with relish.

"Yeah, jist the way you like it," Tuck replied with a note of misgiving in his voice.

"Now Tuck, not everybody's as satisfied t' be in the middle o' nowhere, with nothin' but miles o' nothin', like you."

"Ain't never been insulted, hit, bit, stabbed, 'r shot, by miles o' nothin' but nothin'. An you know I hate towns." Tuck stated flatly.

"Well, if you'd learn t' b'have yerself in these places, things like that wouldn't be a happenin' to ya." Jim chided.

"It ain't me I'm worried about," Tuck replied, giving Jim a mildly reproving sidelong glance. Jim was a social rowdy. He gained energy from those around him and loved to laugh and carouse.

There were about twenty noisy cowhands in the saloon. Some stood at the bar while others occupied tables and played cards. There was no music playing nor shrill laughter from barroom women, just the raucous din of twenty cowhands drinking up their wages and trying to force their way into the only good time to be had in Crayt.

The strangers were an obvious distraction as they entered the saloon and approached the bar. Within moments however, all the cowhands were back to the conversations they had been previously enjoying

Tuck and Jim ordered, greeting Jack cordially.

Jim was soon engaged in a conversation with the cowboy on his left. Tuck stood resting his elbow on the bar and facing the crowd.

Nine cowboys sat at two tables pushed together in the corner. Their tables were already covered with empty beer and shot glasses. They were in high spirits and making considerably more than half of all the noise being made. One cowhand sat at the end of the tables with the others seated along the sides. Tuck noted that the other men seemed to follow the lead of the cowhand at the end.

Jack stopped momentarily from his busy night to point out the nine men to Tuck. Amidst the roar of laughter and conversation he said, "Vogel's hands," and went quickly to serve a tray of drinks.

Tuck spent the next hour just observing and listening.

Jim was beginning to loosen up, as Jim always did, and was entertaining several cowhands gathered at the bar by telling jokes and swapping lies with them.

As Tuck continued his observations one of the cowhands that had been seated with the nine moved to a different table and sat alone.

Shortly, the cowhand who had occupied the space at the head of the tables joined him. Tuck could see they were engaged in earnest conversation. The man who apparently led the group appeared to be admonishing the other on some account.

Before long the cowhand who had been seated by himself became angry and shouted defiantly in a thick southern drawl, "Ah don't give a dang! By thunder, we oughta do somethin' about it!" The older cowhand looked around quickly and ordered the other to keep his voice down. Few in the bar took note but Tucker Spence noted the remark well.

The angry cowboy got up from his table and moved to the bar. The other rejoined the group saying something to them that caused them all to turn and look momentarily at the young man at the bar.

Tuck had been standing away from the crowd gathered by Jim and when the young cowboy came to the bar he stood in the space between Jim and Tuck. He had carried his drink with him and stood staring sullenly down at the glass. After a few minutes, the young man said to no one in particular, "Nuts to 'em, anyway. Ah don't need no grief like that."

"Like what?" Tuck inquired.

The young cowboy turned to look at Tuck for a

few moments.

Then, without saying anything, returned to his perusal of the glass on the bar. Tuck remained silent hoping to draw the boy out.

When the cowboy ventured nothing further Tuck continued.

"Prob'ly a matter o' principle I'd bet. Most people nowadays don't respect men o' principle an' honor. Kinda gets me riled sometimes."

"Worse'n that," the young man muttered without looking at Tuck.

Again Tuck made no immediate reply allowing the cowboy to volunteer his conversation if he would. Several more minutes passed and the cowboy ordered another shot. Tuck minded his business in silence watching the eight men at the table and the ninth at the bar.

"Whar ah'm from they'd hang any coward treat a woman like that... after they castrated him!" The young man spat the words contemptuously. His speech was becoming slurred with drink and his drawl more pronounced.

At the cowhand's remark the hair on Tuck's neck tingled and he could sense the adrenalin rush in his system. It was the chemistry that made some men turn and run like rabbits and others turn and fight. It was a sensation he'd felt many times.

During the war and in the years since the war, the words of Ed Spence about not returning home in a pine box never left Tuck's head. Tuck had come to realize that he possessed a particular skill. In the Army his best friend had been extremely capable in the handling of a pistol from holster to target. He had instructed Tuck and the two practiced constantly whenever there was an opportunity.

Tuck also came to realize that his nerves did not desert him when he was confronted with danger. It was as if the danger sharpened his senses and rather than becoming panicky, he found himself cold and calculating with an inner fury waiting to explode.

Tuck's first uncontrollable experience with it came when he was just a youth in the war and he'd witnessed his best friend's face destroyed by rebel shot. Many had turned and ran that day. Something within Tuck had overcome him for the first time. He experienced uncontrolled fury.

He had charged forward with reckless abandon, the hooves of his mount drumming beneath him. He hadn't looked to see, nor had he cared, if other cavalrymen were charging with him. Only when he found himself among the enemy did he realize he alone had charged. He'd emptied his pistol in the first moments of the engagement and was soon dragged from his horse by Rebel soldiers.

It had been an injudicious act of bravery. He spent the rest of his days until the war ended as a prisoner.

Since that day Tuck had learned to control this overwhelming urge to action until the time was right.

The mention of a woman's mistreatment, and he was sure who the victim was, had triggered an automatic reaction in him. Tuck's knuckles were white as his fingers squeezed the handle of his colt. He took a deep breath and relaxed his grip. He cleared his throat and took a sip of beer.

"Where're ya from?" Tuck asked, trying to make his interest seem casual.

The young cowhand searched Tuck's face with bleary eyes, then said with a touch of pride, "Ah'm from Tennessee. Whar we larn t' treat women an' horses with more respect th'n these ign'rnt forn'rs 'n Yankees 'round here ever knew 'r ever will know. Whar'r you from?"

"I'm from a lotta places now... But, I was born an' lived on a farm in Missouri til I went off t' the war."

"Which side?" the young man demanded.

Tuck smiled calmly at the young cowboy. "Sides don't matter now. Yer way too young fer that war, if ya was even born yet. I don't know that it settled much then, but I certainly know talkin' about it in saloons now won't change 'r settle what happened fer either side."

Tuck moved quickly to change the subject. "Who's doin' what t' ladies 'n horses that's got ya so riled up?"

"Well ah'll tell ya one thing... it don't do t' git me riled! Us Tennessee boys don't cotton t' no Yankees... let alone no dang forn'r Yankee, messin' 'round."

"Which foreigner Yankee is that?"

"The one thet's a cruel coward an' oughta have 'is butt shot off!" The young man was becoming more animated and, as the liquor took effect, less inhibited.

"Why don't ya jus' do it?" Tuck baited.

The young man looked at the table where the

other eight were seated. "Cuz o' them... ah'd have t' kill 'em all. They jus' in it fer money, food, an' a bunk. Give 'em that, they'd work fer the devil... 'n ah think we do."

Tuck watched as the cowboy seated at the head of the table arose and approached them at the bar. He was tall and lanky, older than the hands with him, and walked with a swagger.

When he arrived at the bar he placed his arm around the shoulders of the cowboy from Tennessee. The young man looked up and shrugged the arm from around him. "Take 'er easy Nate... I think you'd mebbe better head fer the barn," the older man said. He looked affably at Tuck and said, "Ole Nate's only been out here 'bout six months... guess Tennessee whiskey ain't as rough on ya as the stuff we git out here."

Tuck eyed the cowboy evenly and said, "He's been tellin' me somethin' real interestin'... says ya work fer a foreigner that don't know how t' treat ladies 'r horses. Any truth t' that?"

The cowboy looked at Tuck with mild surprise and then replied contemptuously, "First off, Nate don't know squat, he's drunk... Second off, what difference is it t' you what a man does on his own ranch with his own stock?"

Tuck felt the anger begin anew and fought for control. "Well, since ya asked me, real polite an' all, I'll tell ya. First off, if a man mistreats horses it makes 'em mean 'n crazy. An' since I buy horses, if they've been mistreated, I don't want 'em. Second, it ain't much of a man that'd mistreat animals, an' less o' one that'd try to prove he is a man by abusin' women. Even less a man th'n that'd watch 'im do it an' not kick his butt fer it. How 'bout that?" Tuck stared hard at the cowboy in an unmistakably invitational manner.

The cowboy returned Tuck's stare for a moment. "Well ya see, ain't none o' that happenin' that I know of, so it don't make nothin' t' me now does it? Nate! Go git on yer horse, yer through in town t'nite."

The young cowboy called Nate spun around angrily to face the older cowhand. "Who 'r you Race t' be a tellin' me when ah'm done in town?"

Race slapped Nate open handed across the face with a resounding crack. A hush fell as the fracas gained the attention of everyone.

"That's jus' fer openers Nate. If ya want more you jus' sass off yer mouth t' me agin." Nate stood glaring at Race with both fists clenched seething with hatred and fury. He swung. It was a wide roundhouse aimed at Race's head. Race saw it coming and fended it off easily. He drove a straight right hand deep into Nate's midsection. The air in Nate's lungs rushed out with a groan. Nate crumpled to the floor wrapping both arms around his abdomen and drawing his knees to his chest. His eyes were wide with surprise and he gasped for air but the wind had been knocked out of him. Race drew back a boot intending to continue his assault.

Jim stepped in quickly and pushed Race roughly aside. He stooped down and rolled Nate over. Forcing Nate's knees down, he pulled on his belt arching Nate's back in the process. Jim repeated the move.

Suddenly Nate gasped in a breath and Jim released him.

When Jim straightened up, Race stepped squarely in front of him. Still primed by his triumph over Nate, he said, "When I want yer interference Jackass, I'll ask fer it."

Jim smiled at Race. "Now ain't you a rooster... all puffed up cuz ya whipped a boy."

"Well now, you ain't no boy are ya? An' from the looks o' things, ya ain't been one in quite awhile." Race hurled.

Jim laughed again, but it wasn't humor. There was the distinct sound of menace. Jim answered Race with an edge to his voice, but Jim was still smiling. "Why no sir, I ain't no boy. An' it's danged observant of ya t' notice. On the other side o' yer comment, it's also been awhile since I stomped the liver out've a little piss ant like you... an' t' tell ya the truth we N'Orleans boys do like t' practice that once in awhile."

Tuck stepped in between Jim and Race. Addressing Race, he said, "Son, I'm gonna give you some advice. He's laughin' but he ain't amused. Let it be."

"What're you his big brother? If he needs protection why don't he git his momma in here, if he's got one," Race retorted, his face mottled with anger.

Tuck shook his head and stepped aside.

The seven other cowhands had surrounded the scene. Race, encouraged by their presence, said, "Me 'n the boys might jus' see who gits stomped, huh boys?"

"All these boys want is fer you to quit playin' the fool and git on outa here, right boys?" It was Jack from behind the bar. "We ain't had no serious problems in this saloon and we don't want none. This's gittin' outta hand. Now Race, you take yer boys an' git. You've all had more t' drink than's good fer ya."

Race looked at Jack defiantly and then turned to Jim. "Awright, let's me an' you take this outside... jus' you 'n me, howzat? Yer wearin' a pistol. Is it fer looks 'r what?"

Jim's mood of mild amusement shifted abruptly and the expression on his face mirrored the shift. He stood for a moment without reply. His eyes grew hard and cold as he stared at Race whose face was still splotched from anger and whose hand was poised near his sidearm. The bar sounds had fallen silent. The only sounds now were the rain drumming on the roof. Outside in the darkness thunder rumbled in deep bass notes.

Jim's reply, when it finally came, was made slowly and calmly. "B'fore we go, you take a look around ya... take in all ya kin see... cuz when we go out that door you've seen yer last... So, when yer ready to die, you stupid fool, jus' move t' the door."

One of the seven stepped alongside Race and took hold of his gun arm.

"Race, dammit, this ain't no thing to mess in. You don't have t' keep goadin' this thing. Let's jus' git on our horses and go sleep this off."

The color began to drain from Race's face. Alcohol had given him courage for a moment, but like any treacherous friend, it deserted him at the critical time of need. Jim's menacing calm and the very real prospect of death had unnerved Race. He was left with nothing now but the measure of his own courage.

Race had threatened only two other men in his life with gunplay. In both cases, he had known prior to the threat that neither of the men would respond. This time he had overplayed his hand and his mouth had placed him in a deadly situation. Fear was fast overcoming the effects of alcohol and a sobering Race knew he was standing closer to death now than at any other time in his life. Outside the thunder gave forth another long ominous bass roll. His mind was racing. He could see only one chance to get out, if he played it right.

"Yeah, yer right, I'm too drunk. Sometimes I git too mean when I drink," Race began his desperate gamble. Looking at Jim he began his pitiful attempt to shift the mood. "Whadda ya think? Think we oughta jus' wait 'til we're both a li'l more sober?"

The idea of escape had seized Race now. He began artificially slurring his speech and intentionally swaying in an attempt to lend credence to his desperate need for the excuse of inebriation. It was his only chance of a way out.

There was a long icy moment as Jim continued his calm deadly stare at the contemptuous spectacle before him. Except for the sound of the rain, there was silence and no one moved. Every eye was fixed on the pair.

"Well now ya see, I ain't drunk. But, if you think you need t' go home an' nurse on momma now, I think it'd be the smart thing t' do," Jim said derisively.

Having committed to the role, even in the face of Jim's contempt, Race could only continue to play it out. "Tha's right, I need t' go home an' sleep," he said, leaning heavily upon the cowhand who had spoken the words of sense to him. His knees appeared rubbery. It was partly an act and partly in rush relief that his situation was beginning to ease.

The cowhands, except for Nate who had recovered sufficiently to stand at the bar, gathered up their personals and left together. They were all supporting the pretense of Race's drunkenness. They were all glad for the chance to ride away in the rain and the darkness and to be leaving in one piece.

Jim moved to the bar and stood beside Nate. The moment seemed to have passed without effect as he grinned at Nate and said, "You got ugly friends son!"

Jim was holding a glass of whiskey in a steady hand. He glanced sideways at Tuck and asked mischievously, "Ya don't think you could carry me across the street t'night so's I won't get my boots all muddy, do ya?"

Tuck grinned. He was glad the situation didn't have to end in violence. He had no doubt what the outcome would have been. No one was taken in by Race's act. Still, it was good that Jim hadn't had to kill him and ruin their chance to approach Vogel in a more disarming manner as horse buyers.

"Nate's the key we've been waitin' for Jim."

"Good. I'm anxious t' git on with it."

"Me too, but we gotta make sure we do it right the first time. The more we kin find out the better chance we got."

After the encounter in the saloon, the young cowboy Nate had no desire to return to the Vogel ranch. He boarded his horse with Bert and spent the night in the barn with Tuck and Jim.

When morning came it was cool and the sky was dark with rain clouds. The wind rose and fell in gusts bringing the first cool hints of autumn. It was the time of year when temperatures changed unpredictably. A day of discomforting heat could be followed by a plunge in temperature requiring warm clothing. The rain was driven by the wind in irregular smatterings making the day less than inviting for travel.

Nate was up early saddling his horse and preparing to depart.

"Goin' back t' work?" Tuck inquired from his blankets.

"Nope, ah'm gonna git me back t' Tennessee where I shudda stayed... an' whar ah belong."

"Mind answerin' a few questions b'fore ya go?"

"Like what?"

"Well you sure seemed peeved about somethin' that I'm interested in. What did ya mean when ya said somebody oughta do somethin' about it? What's goin' on out there that's made ya mad enough t' ride all the way back t' Tennessee?"

"Well, now thet ah've quit, ah guess it ain't none o' mah concern no more." Nate continued his task, tightening the cinch, and tying on his bedroll.

"Tell ya what though. If they warn't so dang many of 'em, ah'd sure fix Vogel's wagon... the cowardly..." Nate was bent over picking up some small items to be placed in his saddlebags and the last of his comment was inaudible to Tuck.

"You ridin' out fer Tennessee t'day then... without stoppin' by the ranch t' pick up yer belongins?"

"Yeste'day was payday. Ah had m' mind made up long afore this mornin'. Brought everythin' ah needed an' got money in m' pocket. Ah'm ready."

Tuck watched as Nate placed a foot in the stirrup. "What if I wuz t' tell ya that me 'n Jim 'r out here t' take care o' the problem you'd like t' see taken care of."

Nate stood in the stirrup for a moment and then stepped down. He gazed at Tuck questioningly for a moment. "Ah ain't sure ah follow you."

"I'm gonna tell ya somethin'. When I'm done you kin choose... Ride on out, 'r tell me what I'd like t' know b'fore ya ride out. Fair enough?"

"Sounds fair... course ah ain't heared what ya gonna say yet neither."

Tuck related to Nate the circumstances that had brought him and his companion to the western territory and to Crayt. He began with the letter he had received in Wichita where he and Jim had been working with the U.S. Marshall's office as contract deputies.

The letter included a railroad ticket. It was from a Senator named Mason Broome of Kentucky. In the letter he revealed that his wife had been abducted by force more than three years earlier. He told of his failed efforts to locate her until a young cowboy passed through Kentucky to deliver a note from her. She stated that she was being held prisoner by Klaus Vogel. The young cowhand had worked on Vogel's ranch. She had managed to smuggle the note to the cowhand after learning he was returning to Kentucky to manage the family farm for his mother.

Through members of his wife's family, the Senator had heard of Tucker Spence and his prowess as a bounty hunter and one who had recovered several females who had been taken captive by the Indians in the west. He offered to pay Tuck for his services if he would go and bring his wife home.

When Tucker arrived in Kentucky, Mason Broome was able to give him a great many details concerning Klaus Vogel. Through the Senator's investigations he learned that Klaus Vogel had fled his own country to escape trial for torturing and raping two young girls who were distant relatives that he had invited to his estate for the summer.

Klaus fled Germany in disguise having been warned by friends in local government that he had no hope of denial and acquittal. Through the U.S. Marshall's organization it had been simple enough for Senator Broome to locate Tucker Spence.

Mason made it clear to Tuck that cost was no object but that discretion was. Mason admitted that he would have preferred to mount an army, ride out, and annihilate Vogel. However, for the sake of his position, and his wife's name, he must be discreet.

He'd managed to keep her disappearance known to only a few by making excuses that she was ill or visiting her family.

Tucker had seen no good reason for such precautions. Had it been his wife, with money no object, an army was exactly what he'd take, and annihilation would be the inevitable outcome. Tucker thought it likely that Mason Broome was short on nerve and a little too concerned for his image. He told Mason that any arrangements he would make would include his partner Jim Link.

In the days that followed, Mason and Tucker devised the horse buyer's ruse to alleviate suspicions and give them the best chance of rescuing Becky without harm to her. Mason schooled Tuck in the finer points of examining blooded horses.

As an additional incentive, Mason provided him with his pick of mounts from his own stock. Tuck chose a tall muscular buckskin gelding for himself and for Jim he chose a beautifully formed sorrel mare with two white stockings, a white blaze and muzzle.

Had Jim been there, Tuck knew it was the horse he would have selected. It was a horse that fit Jim's penchant for style and flair. Jim admired horses that lent themselves to the overall image he liked to portray.

Tuck, on the other hand, was a man of utility. To him, a horse's capabilities were the most important thing.

The horses were shipped west on the train with Tuck.

The following week he and Jim headed for the Colorado and Wyoming territories riding their new mounts and trailing their own horses as pack animals.

After hearing Tuck's account Nate was eager to provide any information he could. "What kin ah tell ya'll thet'll hep ya?"

Tucker had purposefully left out the details concerning his acquaintance with Becky years before.

"What did ya see that got ya riled?" Jim was up and around now.

Nate began relating to Tuck and Jim his suspicions and concerns. He told of the times he'd heard the woman cry out in the night and beg, "Please don't!"

"Ah figger ah know what he's a tryin' t' make her do. He keeps her locked in the house up there. Hands ain't allowed even close t' the fence except fer the foreman, an' Race, he goes up there once in awhile, but only with Vogel right there. Ah know twice he had meetin's up thar with some other for'ners thet stayed th' night. Thet's when I heard her hollerin' the most. One o' the old hands tole me one time that she tried t' run off. Vogel caught 'er, brought 'er back an' hung 'er up by 'er wrists in the barn. Tore off 'er dress an' whipped 'er with a harness. When he was done 'n saw all the hands lookin' at 'er, he jis' laughed an' turned 'er 'round so she could see 'em lookin' at 'er. Ah'm glad ah never saw that... I'm sure I'da had t' kill 'im . Only time ah ever seen 'er was when Vogel'd take 'er t' town. She never looked at any of us, an' ah shore don't think anyone ever talked to 'er... we jus' heard them screams at night."

"What else? Anything?" Jim asked.

Tuck would have asked but his throat was thick with rage and the words would not come.

"Well he's a mean and cruel idiot t' his horses too. He once took a sword thet he sometimes wears an' hamstrung a horse that had kicked at 'im. It ain't nuthin' fer him t' beat a horse with a whip til the horse's dang neart crazy with fear an' cryin' in pain... he likes that... fer folks 'n animals t' be afraid of 'im."

"Is there anythin' we need t' look out fer when we git out there? Seems obvious his foreman's got no spine for fightin'," Jim asked, contemptuous of the thought of the spineless Race.

"Race? Ya mean him? He ain't no foreman. He's jis' been with Vogel longer'n anyone else... he thinks he's somebody... but he ain't nothin' but a hand like us."

"But you did say he has a foreman," Jim questioned.

"Yeah, Soto. He's mean an' low, jis' like Vogel, two of a kind. He's Mexican 'r Indian, mebbe both 'r more... Vogel's big 'n powerful 'n mean an' if ya ask me off in 'is head... but Soto... he's... ah don't know what you'd call it... he's a killer 'n ya don't have t' be round 'im long t' see it. Ah don't know how good you fellers fight... but that's the one t' watch."

After gleaning from Nate information about the house, the grounds, the distances between buildings, and the ways to approach unseen, they thanked him and bid him farewell.

Nate mounted and rode off.

Tuck stared out the barn door for a long time in the direction that Nate rode. When the fury in him finally began to abate he turned to Jim.

"Think we've waited long enough."

Tuck wondered what effect Nate's revelations had made on Jim. With Jim it was hard to tell. He could look disinterested, or, act like he was having a good time, even in tight situations.

Jim glanced over and noticed that Tuck was gazing at him questioningly.

"Let's don't have any real long conversations when we git there, okay Tuck?"

Tuck nodded. He had his answer.

"We'll wait 'n see if the weather clears by afternoon. If it don't we'll ride out anyway. We need t' git a look at the setup out there firsthand if we can. I'd like t' git her out safe first if we can. After that, somebody's gonna pay... an' you'n me'll be the ones collectin'."

Jim was honing the knife that he normally wore in a sheath on his belt behind his back. He used long, rhythmic, slicing, strokes on the stone. In the gloom of the morning, with the wind gusts driving the rain in sheets, Jim was a spectral figure seated in the dimly lit interior of the barn intent upon his task.

When he was finished with the honing, Jim stropped the blade on the leather rein of a harness hanging on the barn wall. He held the knife up to the available light to examine the edge. Satisfied, he rolled up his sleeve and shaved a small patch of hair from the back of his forearm.

"Yessir, the Colt .45 and the Louisiana skinnin' knife, a mighty fine pair, an' Vogel, you woman and animal beating low-life, scum sucker, I can't wait t' introduce ya t' both of 'em."

The rain worsened as the day progressed and by afternoon the two were faced with a long ride in a driving rainstorm.

"Doubt if we'd be able t' sell ourselves off as horse buyers if we hit that ranch in this. Even if it lets up some later, we'd be arrivin' way after dark. Much as I'd like t' git to it we're gonna haf t' wait 'til t'morrow," Tuck said, "I hate t' leave 'er out there another night, but, if we're gonna be able t' git 'er out without runnin' the chance o' havin' t' shoot our way out with her in the path, we need t' wait an' git a layout in broad daylight."

CHAPTER 9

In the morning the two men mounted and rode out in the direction of the Vogel ranch. Sometime during the night the rain had stopped. Neither of them spoke as they rode along.

Tuck had made their plans the night before. They would observe the layout as they looked the horses over. According to Nate, most of what they needed to see could be observed from the corral. After reconnoitering the situation they would ride out of sight and wait until dark. At midnight they would gain entry into the house if possible, by force if they had to, and take Becky safely into their custody.

Jim didn't seem to think much of the plan and favored a more direct approach. He reminded Tuck that things seldom went along quite that smoothly. But, he was prepared for whatever it took to get the job done.

It was nearly noon when they crested the first

hill that allowed a visual sighting of the ranch house and outbuildings. They stopped to eat and to survey the ranch from their vantage point before riding in.

Tuck was vexed within himself. He couldn't keep his mind from wandering to things that were only getting in the way of his concentration on the plan. He was inwardly embarrassed by his petty concern for what Becky would say or do at first sight of him. Would she throw herself upon him when she realized it was he who had come for her? Should he kiss her? He knew a more important concern was whether he was going to have to shoot his way in or out, but Becky filled his thoughts.

As if that were not enough, his mind strayed to the final days of the war when he and Jim were prisoners held aboard a prison ship near the mouth of a river in South Carolina.

They had formed an alliance in those days determining to survive and see freedom.

They vowed to be partners for life if they ever got out of that Hell. Together they had overcome the depression of prison clinging to the dream of someday having a ranch together.

It was by sheer luck that they had determined to work their way into a couple of horses and ride out of the South rather than allow the Army to provide transportation home and return to Tuck's father's place in Missouri. On the way up the Mississippi from New Orleans to St. Louis, carrying Union troops that had been former prisoners of the Confederacy, a steamboat called the steam driven paddle wheeler SS Sultana had exploded. Only 25% of the 2427 passengers on board survived. When they heard the news, they felt as if they had once again cheated death.

These experiences bound the two men together as close as any brothers. It was at this time that they discussed their plans that, should they ever find the right women to marry, they would raise their families on one spread large enough to provide for everyone.

However, a couple of years working on a ranch after the war revealed that the routine of ranching held no fascination for either of them.

A different line of work seemed more fitting for the skills of the two. Both Tuck and Jim were expert gun handlers. They put this asset to work.

Immediately after the war, there were still those individuals who either had taken, or were still taking, advantage of war widows and the families of the men who had failed to come home for whatever reasons. Homesteads and ranches were being taken over, robbery and looting was a frequent occurrence, and in many cases it was by men who themselves had not served in the war, but had been a scourge on the populace while the men were away fighting.

There were many of these men who had prices on their heads. Tuck and Jim saw that bringing these outlaws to justice was obviously better pay and a whole lot less hard labor than ranching. They were sometimes deputized by the local sheriffs, but were never part of the vigilante groups who ran about masked and disguised becoming as much a terror as those they were supposedly bringing to justice.

Tuck and Jim's view was: they wanted the outlaws to understand there were decent men in the territory who were not going to abide preying upon the weak and the innocent. If they wanted to be bad men, then they needed to learn there were always men who can and will be as bad as necessary to stop them. They wanted them to look death in the face and then see how bad they thought they were. Most of the men they pursued were caught on the run, but there were a few who made the fatal mistake of standing their ground.

Something triggered Tuck's mind back to reality. *What if something happened to Jim?* In the next moment he was wondering what if after all this time Becky wanted to rekindle that old romance?

Tuck was confused by his own feelings and frustrated by his inability to concentrate and sort things in order of importance. He knew what was most important. He just couldn't discipline his mind to observe the precedence of things.

As the two men rode through the first gate leading to a small concentration of buildings ahead Jim began to softly hum a tune. He was easing tension. Sometimes when Jim got tense he became unpredictable, never unreliable, but unpredictable.

Tuck and Jim sat astride their horses and studied the stock inside the corral. No one acknowledged their presence. In fact, no one seemed to be around.

Just as Tuck decided to ride up to the house, the barn door opened and Race stepped out. Seeing the two startled him and he closed the doors behind him in haste looking around in confusion.

"What're you two doin' here?"

"We came t' see Vogel about buyin' some horses," Tuck replied.

Jim sat on his horse in silence, gazing disinterestedly at Race.

"Well, he's inside... stay here... I'll go in an' tell 'im."

Jim walked his horse around the outer perimeter of the corral looking over the stock again. At one point he stood up in his stirrups, shading his eyes with his hat against the sun, in order to see something across the corral on the side of the barn that was obscured from Tuck's view.

Race returned, followed by two men. One was obviously Klaus Vogel. He was, as Nate had described, a huge man with broad shoulders and an immediately noticeable arrogant bearing. Vogel was openly hostile and glared at Tuck as an intruder. He was definitely not in the mood for business.

The other man was a small wiry Mexican who had about a dozen black hairs on his upper lip where a mustache should have been, pox marks in his face, bad teeth, and an equally hostile and contemptuous countenance. He wore a pistol on his right hip with the holster tied down and he had another stuck in the waistband of his trousers.

Tuck pretended not to notice their obvious agitation.

"Howdy. My pardner an' me 'r horse buyers. We heard ya had some o' the best stock in the territories... wanted t' come an' see what ya got... judge if they'd be worth buyin' an' shippin' back t' improve our boss's line."

Vogel eyed him for a moment without speaking. His square jaw jutted from a severe face that sported an aquiline nose which to Tuck looked like an open invitation for a hard fist. Tuck controlled himself. Few things provoked him more than another man's arrogance.

"Ve don't haf time today! Ve are busy vit other matters! Vy did you not mek arrangements in advance?"

Jim had just returned from looking the corral over. He walked his horse up close beside the men on the ground. He had his left forearm resting on the saddle horn and the thumb of his right hand resting on his gunbelt just above the grip of his Colt. "Listen jackass! Ya better git off yer high horse an' talk in a civil manner, cuz there's lotsa things in this world that we ain't used to, nor ever will abide, an' takin' sass is chief among 'em!"

Jim's voice was hard and his menace unmistakable. Tuck could see the plan going by the wayside in a hurry. Jim's aggression was a sure indicator that he intended to force the issue here and now.

"Hey, Gringo!" Soto spat at Jim. "Jou wan' to step down off jour horse an' let me see how…"

The explosion of Jim's Colt occurred with such suddenness that it took Tuck by surprise and he fought to control his mount. Soto was slammed back against the barn wall, his eyes wide in astonishment, and a bullet hole in his chest.

In the next instant Jim backhanded the barrel of the Colt across Vogel's face and Tuck watched as the nose shattered. Vogel reeled backward with Jim in murderous pursuit. Jim sprang from the saddle with the agility of a cat and in his left hand he held the knife. Vogel screamed in desperation and leaped back through the barn door. He slammed the door closed and dropped the locking bar in place. Out of the corner of his eye Tuck saw Race drawing his pistol with a clear shot at Jim's back. Tuck's Colt roared to life and the opposite side of Race's skull splattered against the barn.

In a matter of seconds they saw the fleeing Vogel, riding his mount bareback, heading for open country.

"Jim! He just rode out the back door!"

Before Tuck could continue, Jim grabbed the reins of Tuck's horse. "We can get him when we want him." Jim led him around the side of the barn and pointed to a figure swinging at the end of a rope, hanged by the neck from a loading arm that protruded from the loft. "That's Nate."

Aware of a sound behind them, Tuck whirled his horse. The other cowhands were coming from the bunkhouse approaching the scene. They were sullen but seemed greatly relieved to see the two men alive and two of their former bosses dead.

The cowboy who had talked sense to Race in the saloon stepped forward. He pointed to the figure hanging at the barn. "They caught him an' drug him back in the rain yesterday... it was god awful... They kept at him most of the night. Hung him this mornin'... made us watch. When ya hire on they tell ya yer horse is yers. Nate believed 'em. After he left they said that only applied if ya still worked here... said Nate knew that just like we did and that Nate was a horse thief. Don't take ya long workin' here to realize that it don't pay t' speak up against 'em. We never figured they'd go after him in the rain... but they did."

Tuck looked at the men gathered in the group and realized that each of them had been a prisoner of fear on the ranch. "You boys git yer stuff packed up. Pick out yer horse an' one fer a pack animal if ya need it. You've paid fer 'em workin' here."

Tuck asked a question next that almost stuck in his throat. "The woman up in the house still alive?"

The men looked at one another, shook their heads, or shrugged their shoulders, to indicate that they didn't know. "Should we bury 'em?" one of the men asked, looking at the two dead men lying on the ground.

"Leave 'em. Bury Nate."

Tuck turned his horse toward the house. Glancing at Jim he asked, "You comin?"

"No. You go on... I'm gonna take care o' Nate."

Tuck rode through the gate and up the lane to the house. He tied his horse at the rail, ascended the porch steps, opened the massive front door, and entered the huge house.

The interior was elegantly furnished. The great room looked warm and inviting giving no indication of the fiendish nature of its owner.

He stood still for a moment listening for a sound and heard only his own breathing. He searched the immediate area with his eyes. "Becky!" Tuck called out. There was no reply.

He searched each of the rooms downstairs and found no one. As he climbed the stairs he became apprehensive, afraid of what he might find. There were four rooms each with its door closed.

Tuck opened the door of the first room and found it oddly arranged with several chairs in a semi-circle around a bed.

He tried the door across the hall. By the look of its contents he concluded this had been Vogel's bedroom. The next door was locked. He tried the fourth door and it opened to reveal a room used for storage. He returned to the locked door.

"Becky?" he called. There was no answer. "Becky?" he called again, twisting the knob of the door. "Becky, are ya in there?"

Tuck threw his shoulder against the door. It was a heavy door with a strong lock. He ran against it from across the hall, but the door remained closed and locked. As he looked around for something to use as a battering ram he thought he heard something. He ran back to the door and pressed his ear against it but heard nothing. He waited. "Becky! Are ya in there?"

"Who are you?" came a faint reply.

"It's Tucker Spence, Becky, I've come t' git ya."

"I don't know if Becky's here," came the faint voice again.

Tuck's heart fell. "Who 'r you?" he asked. There was no reply.

Tuck looked around again for something to add its weight and structure to his in order to batter the door down. He ran to a window and saw the wood axe on a block used to chop and split firewood. He raced down the stairs and outside to retrieve it.

When he returned he called to the woman through the door.

"Stay away from the door, I'm gonna have t' break it down."

The door soon splintered under his assault with the axe and he could see a frail figure seated on a bed at the far end of the room. A few more blows and he had gained entry. He stepped quickly over to the small figure seated on the bed. She was wide-eyed and held a bed sheet up to hide her nakedness.

"Don't hurt me... I'll do whatever you want... just don't hurt me... alright? What do you want me to do?"

Tuck's insides turned. He was sure it was Becky. She was pale and thin and stared at Tuck from hollow eyes that projected fear but no sign of recognition.

Tuck looked around the room to find something for her to put on. He remembered a room downstairs that had been full of dresses and female apparel.

When he returned she was still sitting in the same place staring vacantly across the room. She saw the dresses and her eyes brightened. She looked longingly at them, but made no effort to take them. She looked at Tuck with suspicion and a trace of defiance, then returned her gaze to the dresses. Tears began to flow down her cheeks.

Tuck could see that Becky was in a state of mental disarray and though he longed to hold her and assure her, he knew it was not the right time. He laid the dresses across her bed and said as gently as he knew how, "I'll be downstairs... come down when yer ready."

Tuck left the room shaking his head in disbelief. Nothing had been as he had anticipated. He thought he had prepared himself and if she had been dead he would have been better prepared than he was to have found her like this.

Until now, Tuck had been critical of the rash action taken by Jim. Even seeing Nate hanging from the barn had not triggered the kind of reaction in Tuck that Jim had displayed. But, there was rage within him now. Tuck didn't believe in torture. He'd witnessed enough prolonged suffering in prison to last a lifetime. But, he was anxious to get his hands on Vogel.

CHAPTER 10

"Well, it seemed kinda stupid t' me all along... posin' as horse buyers. When I seen all three of 'em right there, I knew she was either alright 'r she wasn't... an' it sure didn't seem t' me there was any need t' play games."

Tuck heard Jim out on the matter. It still galled him some that Jim had taken matters into his own hands. He had to admit that with all three of the people Nate had said could give them a problem standing right there it was the time to act, but Tuck was a man of order and plans.

Tuck dropped the subject when the small figure appeared in the doorway of the great room. She was far too thin for the dress she had donned and her face was drawn and gaunt. Dark circles pronounced the hollowness of her eyes.

Tuck searched her features trying to find the face that had tantalized his thoughts on so many occasions. It was Becky, but age and ordeal had wrought significant changes in her. She looked smaller than he remembered. Her hair was sandy with streaks of blond, not the golden tresses of his dreams. The nose was no longer freckled and the liquid eyes of brown were dull and vacant.

"Where is Klaus?" she asked apprehensively, her eyes suspiciously searching the room. She reminded Tuck of a frightened puppy.

Tuck looked at Jim but Jim made no reply. "He ain't gonna hurt you ever again," Tuck said.

"Dead?" she asked, her tone suspicious.

"No, but he will be" Tuck replied flatly.

If Becky believed him, or understood the impact of Tuck's comment, nothing showed in her face. "Who are you?" she asked in confusion, as though he had told her once but now she had forgotten.

Her question was like a knife in Tuck's heart. All of the anticipation on the trail to rescue her, day and night, culminated in disappointment by that question. If Becky had changed considerably since he last saw her, maybe he had too. Heartened by the thought Tuck answered, "Tucker Spence, Becky. Remember me?"

She didn't answer.

Jim stepped to Tuck's side and, speaking softly, said, "She's been through a lot Tuck, an' maybe this's time t' jist git on down the trail an' let 'er have some time t' git use to us." Jim turned to the woman and asked, "Becky, we came t' take ya back home. Can ya git yer things t'gether?"

"Where's Klaus?" she asked again. Her eyes searched the room. She still did not trust them.

Jim walked over to her and took both of her hands in his. He spoke tenderly to her, "Becky, look at me." Becky raised her eyes until they met Jim's and she returned his gaze impassively. "Klaus Vogel is gone. He's not here. He won't be near you anymore. Tuck an' me are here t' take ya back home to yer husband. Do ya understand?"

She made no audible reply, but the tears that welled up in her eyes were enough to let Jim know she was beginning to grasp the situation. She squeezed his hands hard and Jim stood waiting for her to make the next move.

Tuck found himself suddenly very uncomfortable with an overwhelming need for fresh air. "I'll git things ready t' go. See if ya kin git 'er packed up with whatever she needs t' go. I'll git a wagon ready." Tuck left the two of them inside.

He was confused and more than a little dejected. It seemed to him that if she were going to respond to anyone, in any way, it would have been to him. Becky's reaction to Jim had produced a reaction in Tuck he wasn't quite sure about.

As he approached the barn, Tuck took note that someone had cleared the bodies away. He entered the barn and discovered an upholstered two-seat carriage and, in the stalls, a matched team of horses.

He soon had the horses harnessed and hitched to the carriage.

Back in the house, a scene had developed that would have proven even more disconcerting for Tuck if he had stayed. Moments after he left, Becky's defensive wall collapsed a little more with the realization that her torment was over. She collapsed against Jim. He held her in his arms as she sobbed her relief against his chest. Jim held her without a word while the flood of tears began their cleansing process.

When her sobs subsided and she relaxed her desperate grasp around his chest, he lifted her chin gently with one hand and softly patted her face with the other. Looking into her eyes reassuringly he said, "It's okay now darlin', nobody's gonna hurt ya. Ole Jim ain't gonna allow it. Ya think ya kin help me git yer things t'gether? We need t' git ya away from here." Her eyes were red from crying but her face was devoid of expression. She nodded in the affirmative and withdrew her arms from around him.

As Tuck drove the carriage to the house he was deep in thought. *She would've had to remember me at least once. It was just that everything she'd been through had put her mind in a state. Given enough time she'll come back to herself.* He'd probably be wise not to push it.

When he arrived at the front of the house, Jim came through the door carrying a large trunk and placed it on the carrier at the back of the carriage.

"I figgered we'd follow the freight trail t' Cheyenne. We kin ship the horses an' take 'er back on the train." Tuck continued, "Has she said anything yet?"

"Not really. I think she's got the idea now though, that it's over," Jim replied. "I went upstairs t' see if there might be somethin' we needed t' take. Did ya see that room with them chairs around the bed?" Without waiting for a reply he continued,

"They do that down in N'Orleans."

Tuck could feel his neck redden. He knew what it was when he saw it. He just didn't want to talk about it. The thought of it was bad enough.

"Now if the hands wasn't allowed up t' the house, an' there was only three of 'em that were... with that many chairs I think I know why Vogel had visitors."

"Jim! I don't wanna talk about it!"

Jim looked up in surprise at Tuck's outburst, shrugged and said, "Well, suit yerself. I'll go git the horses. You drive the buggy, I'll ride."

When Becky finally came out of the house she had a small valise with her. Tuck stepped down to take it from her and helped her step up to the carriage seat.

Jim sat astride his horse at the gate trailing Tuck's mount behind his.

Tuck climbed back into the seat beside Becky, turned the horses, and drove to the gate.

Jim tied the buckskin to the back of the carriage and they headed for Crayt without looking back.

They proceeded for about an hour without talking. Finally Tuck spoke to Becky. "We know ya been through a lot. If ya git hungry, 'r thirsty, jist say somethin', alright? It'll be purty late when we git t' town."

Her hands were folded in her lap as she sat with her shoulders drooped forward staring at the dashboard. She nodded in the affirmative. They rode on in silence.

They would reach Crayt a good while after dark. The wind was brisk and the onset of autumn brought an invigorating freshness to the night air.

Jim, while riding alongside Becky, had dropped a coat around her shoulders. She'd pulled the coat around her without a word or a glance.

"Jim, why doncha ride on t' the barn an' git us a lantern goin' so we kin git settled in fer the night."

Jim spurred his horse forward.

When the carriage arrived at the barn Jim swung the door open and met them with the lantern.

Tuck unhitched the team and turned them into the corral along with their other horses. He and Jim used the tongue of the carriage to back it into the barn.

"Sorry Becky, this's the best we kin do. You kin make yer bed on the carriage seat, or like me 'n Jim sleep in the straw."

She looked around at her surroundings. Her eyes came to rest on Tuck and she stared questioningly for a moment. "Tucker Spence? From when I was–" she stopped speaking and stared at him with curiosity.

Tuck stepped to her side, patted her hand, and said with a grin, "Yep, the same one."

"I'm hungry," she said. Dullness returned to her eyes. It was as if after briefly connecting with him she'd gone back to whatever state she had been in.

But, for Tuck, it was a delicious moment. She did remember him. Once she was in the barn he reasoned, that moment so many years ago must have come back to her, if only for a second. "I'll go see what Bert kin do."

Tuck headed up the incline to the store. He looked up in fascination at the ink black, star filled, sky. The cold wind possessed just enough bite to make him hurry. He observed to himself what a grand and glorious night it was.

After an early breakfast the three left from Bert's store in the near light of dawn. It would be a three-day trip from Crayt to Cheyenne.

It was a morning every bit as glorious as the night had been. The grass glistened with dew. The wind had died around midnight and the day dawned clear and bright. A brilliant yellow sun beamed from an azure sky and white cottony clouds floated high above. Tuck was driving the carriage with Becky at his side, while Jim was on horseback. The buckskin and the packhorses trailed behind the carriage.

Tuck was reminded of mornings just like this when he and Jim awakened on the trail far from the problems of other people. He hated towns. Tuck loved the trail. He'd often dreamed of living a secluded life far from the factious groups of people who lived in towns. A man had to have an income though. The things he and Jim did best for a living had to be done in towns.

Becky was silent, but responded in visual ways to their occasional comments to her. They assumed she was listening and understood.

They made camp the first night beside a stream whose waters ran swiftly from the recent rain.

Soon the smell of bacon frying and coffee boiling wafted on the night air. "We'll have every Injun within a hun'erd miles invitin' themselves t' supper if they get a whiff o' that," Jim said, partly in jest, but also to remind Tuck that the freight trail led through land that the Cheyenne and Arapaho were known to have used as hunting ground.

Tuck shot a quick glance at Becky to see if the remark had alarmed her. If she had been affected by Jim's remark there was no outward sign.

Tuck motioned for Jim to come out beyond earshot. "You tryin' t' tell me sumthin?"

"Well, I ain't seen nuthin' yet, but, let's jus' say I got a feelin'... we need t' keep a close watch on them hill tops. The way Injuns figger we prob'ly got a way more horses than we need. Not t' mention a woman."

"Yeah I know, Bert said the freight wagons travel armed t' the teeth. But, they haven't had any problems."

Both men carried Winchester repeating rifles and were accomplished marksmen.

Jim had two rifles, a Winchester in a scabbard slung on his saddle and a .50 caliber Remington rolling block that he'd carried for years. It was broken down and tied to his bedroll.

Tuck had asked him once why he carried both rifles. Jim stated that you never knew when you'd need to hit something extra hard. He figured that was a shot for the Remington. Still, firepower was to little avail if you were taken by surprise and overwhelmed. The night passed without incident and they were on the trail very early the next morning.

They had traveled for about two hours when Becky surprised them both with an extremely direct question.

"Who is going to kill Klaus?" She was looking

up at Jim when she blurted out the unexpected query. Jim rode along without answering her for a few moments steadily returning her gaze.

"What difference does it make?" Tuck asked, not defiantly, but with concern, attempting by his tone to suggest that she might be better off to spare herself the concern.

"I want to know!" she demanded in an imperious tone, which when taken together with the withering glance she threw at Tuck, suggested that she'd just as soon decide for herself about the details. She was again looking to Jim for the reply.

"I'll be happy to do it," Jim stated flatly.

Becky suddenly stood upright in the carriage and held her arms out to Jim. Tuck drew the team to a stop as Jim leaned over in the saddle and placed his left arm around her shoulders. She clung tightly to him, arms around his waist, and sobbed for several minutes, her face buried against his shirt. Jim stared off in the distance. Tuck could feel his neck reddening with anger.

When once again the cleansing stream of tears had purged the emotions pent up within her, she withdrew her arms from around Jim. She stood looking at him for just a moment before surprising him with another question. "Can you kill him by yourself?"

Both Jim and Tuck were taken aback by her question. Jim looked questioningly at her for a moment unsure of her implication. Jim Link was a straight ahead kind of man and although he had no idea what the effect would be he answered her truthfully and directly.

"Yes, I reckon I can," Jim replied matter-of-factly.

"Alright then!" she said, as if some great dilemma for her was finally concluded.

She remained standing for a moment longer, smoothed the front of her dress with her hands, turned to glance momentarily and disdainfully at Tuck, and then turned back to Jim. "There will always be a special place in my heart for the man who kills that horrible beast! I want to make sure I love the right man!" She sat back down and stared straight ahead.

Jim's mouth fell open in astonishment. His hand flew to his mouth to suppress a roar of laughter that would have otherwise gushed forth. He instantly spurred his horse and turned off the trail as the increasingly uncontrollable force of hilarity fought to be free. His body convulsed with inward laughter at her amazing remark. Try as he might to suppress any sounds of mirth a few snorts managed to escape his hand. The sound of that made him worse and he continued riding away from the carriage.

He knew he shouldn't laugh because of the circumstances that had obviously affected her reasoning abilities. But, the product of her obscure reasoning he had just witnessed was so absurd he couldn't help himself.

Tuck wasn't laughing. He was hurt, embarrassed, and angry. He urged the team forward with a crisp verbal command. As he drove on in silent frustration he wondered what could possibly be said in reply to Becky's attitude toward him.

Becky remained silent by his side.

About midday, Jim rode up alongside Tuck. Since Becky's outburst he had trailed behind the carriage. He was as confused as Tuck.

"Wanna stop up here by the trees an' eat somethin'?"

"I s'pose," Tuck mumbled in reply.

Tuck really didn't want to stop. As long as they kept going Becky was content to stare straight ahead and Tuck wasn't anxious for another confrontation.

Tuck pulled the carriage off the trail under the shade of the tree that Jim had indicated. The noonday sun was warm and bright. However, Tuck's melancholy precluded any appreciative observance of the day similar to the one that he'd enjoyed a few hours earlier.

Jim had dismounted and was spreading the blanket from his bedroll on the ground in the grass. He motioned for Becky to occupy the blanket. Without a word she walked over to be in the shade of the tree but did not sit down. Jim divided the contents of a package of food prepared the morning before at Bert's store.

Tuck busied himself around the horses adjusting harness on the team and packs on the packhorses. He was talking softly to the buckskin, patting the horse on the neck, when Jim touched his arm to gain his attention.

"Do ya feel sumthin'... I don't know... jist somethin' strange?"

"Ya mean stranger than her?" Tuck replied with unveiled frustration.

"I ain't talkin' 'bout her. I mean it's like bein' watched but I can't see nobody."

"I seen 'em."

"When? Where?" Jim asked as he glanced around at the surrounding terrain. "Was it Injuns?"

"Don't know, but if ya had yer mind more on what's goin' on an' a little less on how t' shine up t' Becky, you'da seen 'em yerself."

Jim stepped back and eyed Tuck quizzically for a moment seeking in vain for an indication that he was joking.

Tuck remained attentive to the Buckskin.

Jim shook his head in bewilderment. Traveling with a woman who was totally out of touch with reality, regardless of the circumstances that placed her in such a state, was enough to contend with. Now Tuck was unraveled about her misplaced attention. The woman was obviously incapable of directing her attention, or anything else, with any clear logic.

"Tuck, I think ya need t' give that woman some time. Her head ain't right yet, an' it might never be. An' you kin go t' Hades if ya think I care who 'r what she thinks about. On the other hand, I do care about my hair an' my behind. So if you see sumthin' again I'd 'preciate knowin' about it."

They were soon back on the freight road to Cheyenne. For the remainder of the afternoon Becky seemed content to ride along silently. Tuck was content to let her.

Jim trailed behind them on the sorrel mare. Tuck's accusation had caused Jim to feel a small pang of guilt. He had to admit his mind had produced a couple of foolish thoughts about the woman who, after all, was another man's wife. The problem was she wasn't Tuck's wife either, and in Jim's eyes, Tuck had been acting the fool over her from the beginning. He hoped he could avoid problems with Tuck. He'd never seen him act like this.

Tuck was angry with himself. He hadn't seen anyone or anything except Becky and Jim. He simply had misgivings toward Jim and when the opportunity came to make him look foolish he couldn't help himself. If anyone had been preoccupied it was he and not Jim. The facts were that Tuck knew in his heart he was making a fool of himself over Becky. He fully realized that after her ordeal he was expecting too much. He knew it, but was having problems dealing with it. Now, he had lied to his partner.

The gathering around the fire that evening was silent. Becky was lost somewhere within herself and the two men simply avoided conversation.

Jim pulled his bedroll well away from the embers. If something happened he wanted to be sure his eyes were already adjusted to darkness. He was fatigued after riding all day, but he had learned to trust his instincts. He slumbered lightly continually rousing himself. Sleeping without a blanket, the crisp night air prevented him from entering a deep sleep.

Sometime after midnight Jim's instincts gave alarm. His eyes flew open wide and he lay on his blankets listening for the slightest sound. His senses bristled with cautious anticipation. A dark figure in the pale moonlight moved ever so slightly near the area where Becky slept.

Jim waited and watched. Was it Tuck? Tuck wouldn't sneak around his own camp, unless he was trying to cozy up to Becky without waking her or Jim. In the moment of Jim's indecision a rifle shot cracked in the night. The muzzle flash came from the carriage. The figure in the dark flew backwards and skidded across the campfire sending sparks showering. Becky's fearful scream pierced the night.

Men's voices and horses running could be heard in the darkness, the drumming of their hooves fading rapidly in the distance. Jim's eyes strained to penetrate the night as he held his breath listening for any close discernible sound.

"Jim!" Tuck called out. Tuck's voice came from the location of the muzzle flash and Jim was relieved to know that the figure that had crashed to the ground was not his partner.

"I'm here!" Jim replied immediately.

They both waited in the dark listening. Only the rustling sounds caused by the gentle night breeze could be heard. Then Jim heard footsteps near the fire.

"Becky?" Jim shouted attempting to identify her whereabouts if it became necessary to fire in that direction.

"She's not hurt," Tuck replied, his voice coming from the direction of the campfire.

Jim hurried to the spot to find Becky sitting up but making no sound. Tuck was kneeled down examining the intruder.

"Jim, put some stuff on the fire, will ya? We need t' git a look at this. Whoever wuz with 'im rode off."

It took a moment for the added grass and dry weeds to catch fire and create enough light to distinguish any details. Tuck had dragged the body closer to the fire. As the flickering light grew in intensity it revealed a middle aged man, apparently an Indian or half-breed, with a hole in his chest and blood soaking the front of a checkered shirt. He wore a buckskin overshirt, breeches, and moccasins. A Remington Navy revolver was stuck in his belt.

Tuck had pried a knife from the man's grip and held it up to the firelight so Jim could see it.

"Ya think they wuz after the horses Tuck?"

"No I don't. They'd been watchin' us long enough t' know the horses were tethered behind the buggy. He came from the other side o' the camp right straight t' her."

"When did ya' pick 'em up?"

"Well, I had t' go see mother nature, so I walked out behind the rig an' I seen 'em crossin' the trail out there in the moonlight big as ya please. They rode all the way aroun' the camp an' then he come in from that side. I jist got up in the seat an' waited fer 'em."

It would only be natural for Jim to assume that these were the men Tuck had claimed to see earlier. "How many was there? An' why didn't ya git me up?"

"Why, I knew an ole gun hand like you wasn't gonna git slipped up on... was ya?" Tuck looked at Becky and grinned, delighting in this opportunity to point out that it was he and not Jim who had saved her. "I counted four horses when they crossed the trail."

If Becky noticed Tuck's display she made no indication. She had been silent since her scream of fright when shocked from sleep by Tuck's Winchester. "Who is that?" she finally stammered.

"We ain't got no idea," Jim responded.

Jim and Tuck searched the man's pockets for anything that might give them a clue as to who or what he was. Jim removed the Remington from the man's belt and stuck it in his own.

"You ain't gonna carry that are ya?" Tuck asked in reference to the heavy revolver.

"No, but he don't need it. I'll put it on a packhorse. Why, do you want it?" Jim offered.

"Why didn't he come himself?" Becky asked disgustedly.

Her question came as a surprise to both men. Tuck and Jim both looked at the dead man while they pondered her question. Finally, they both looked at each other and shrugged, neither of them quite sure what she'd meant.

"I s'pose he figgered there was safety in numbers," Jim ventured, still puzzled by her question.

"Not him!" she shouted angrily at Jim, pointing to the dead man on the ground beside the fire.

"Well who the heck ya talkin' about then?" Jim's question came sharply to this woman who, in his opinion, seldom made sense.

Tuck was inwardly pleased that Jim was on the receiving end of her venom this time.

"I'm talking about my husband you... idiot!"

Her face, in the firelight, reflected anger and frustration as she lashed out verbally at Jim.

Jim rose to his feet and looked coldly down at the quarrelsome woman. He took a moment to compose himself and then addressed himself to Tuck. "She ain't right and with a mouth like that she's lucky she ain't," Jim exclaimed. He stomped back to his bedroll outside the firelight, glad to be away from this strange and aggravating woman.

Tuck dragged the body a great distance from the camp. Without a shovel, and in the dark, there wasn't much else he could do.

Now, he thought, she won't be so high on Jim. She knows when it comes to protection I can hold my own.

When Tuck returned to the fire Becky was sitting upright with her arms encircling her blanketed knees. It was a picture that triggered a moment in time many years before and Tuck was moved by the recollection.

"Do you know what Klaus Vogel did to me?" she asked. Her eyes were narrow slits in the light of the fire and the words hissed from her lips.

"I think I got a purty good idea," Tuck replied, wishing to avoid this line of conversation.

"Do you!?... do you think you have a pretty good idea!?" Her voice was shrill and choked with emotion.

Before Tuck could tell her that he really didn't think he needed to know, she continued.

When Becky finished relating the humiliating details of her ordeal she dropped her head on her knees and sobbed mournfully.

Tuck was wilted in his spirit after hearing the extent of her sufferings.

Vogel had forcibly degraded her in ways that were only mentioned in the back alleys of seaports. She had been used on many occasions to entertain his guests. Some who spoke no English, expressed their desires in German to Vogel and he, in turn, commanded her in English to obey. It seemed he found his greatest pleasure through domination. It gave Klaus sick satisfaction to force her to do his bidding against everything she wished or believed.

Tuck was glad when Becky finally lay back on her blankets and sobbed herself to sleep. He had known that a time would come when he would have to face the knowledge of what he and Jim already suspected.

He knew what she'd gone through and he was sickened by it. Still her rejection of him was painful. He was confused about his feelings. On the one hand, he wanted to build an emotional barrier against her to avoid the pain of her indifference. But on the other, he wanted desperately to comfort her. If her plight had been torture for him to listen to, what must it have been for her to live through? He drifted off to sleep wrapped in his blankets with visions in his mind that he wished he didn't have.

In the morning, Jim rolled the half-breed's body in a blanket and tied it over the back of his sorrel mare. He and Tuck had agreed that the best thing would be to turn it over to the sheriff in Cheyenne. The fact that the half-breed had been bent on killing or taking Becky and not the horses still bothered them. Klaus Vogel was probably the force behind all of this. They thought perhaps the sheriff might know the man.

Tuck was silent and sullen as he went about the chores of breaking camp and getting ready for the trail. The conversation of the night before had destroyed all illusions that Tuck may have had. He saddled the buckskin and as they left camp he fell in several yards off to the left of the trail lost in his own thoughts.

Jim drove the carriage.

Tuck mulled things over in his mind throughout the morning. He was left with nothing but confessions. He had to confess that if he hadn't been so eager to believe in Tucker Spence, the great deliverer, he wouldn't have had the expectations that he'd had. That confession hurt. He had to confess that he had been pretty foolish to think that after all of these years that Becky would have feelings for him. Last, he had to confess he'd never been so frustrated in all of his life.

As they steadily closed the distance to Cheyenne, with Jim beside Becky, she offered no conversation. But, Jim sensed a difference in her. Tears were often streaming down her face. An important catharsis had begun.

They arrived in front of the sheriff's office just before dark. Tuck went inside and soon returned with the sheriff and his deputies. The deputies removed the body from Jim's mare and carried it to the undertaker's office.

At the livery, Tuck had negotiated a fair price for the carriage, harness, and team. He pressed the money into Becky's hand after escorting her to the hotel. "Ya might need somethin'. Git a hot bath an' a good night's sleep. We'll see ya in the mornin'." She took his arm for a moment, looked into his eyes with what he sensed as an apologetic look, then turned and ascended the stairs.

Without her knowledge, Tuck had made arrangements for one of the deputies to spend the night outside her door. He hadn't forgotten the incident on the trail. It felt good to be able to think straight again. He knew that for too long his mind had been cluttered with vanities and foolish imaginations.

Jim stood in the doorway of the hotel with a broad grin on his face.

"Gamin' tables, drinks to lift the spirit, an' females that didn't come t' argue await us ole friend."

Tuck laughed and clapped Jim on the shoulder. Things were quickly becoming right again.

"Lead on m' friend, not that you ever needed encouragement."

"Its good t' see ya laugh again. Ya ain't laughed much lately," Jim remarked.

"Yeah, well Tucker Spence's been out ridin' a strange trail fer awhile. Its time he got back on the right one."

The two friends left the hotel and headed for the nearest saloon.

CHAPTER 11

The Eagle's Nest was a thoroughly impressive saloon. Three large crystal chandeliers were suspended from a ceiling finished in hardwood panels. The walls were ornamented with alternating panels of mirrors and landscape paintings. Lighted oil wick lamps with multi-colored glass globes were mounted on the upright beams that separated each wall panel. They cast a festive glow over the interior. The long massive bar was polished mahogany with a brass foot rail running the entire length. Polished tables and chairs were situated throughout the room.

In the early 1800s, cattle barons, gold miners and sheep ranchers in the area were among the richest people in the world. They demanded luxurious appointments in their watering holes, bordellos and opera houses. One such was *The Cheyenne Club* known to have a library the equal to nearly any place in the world.

The *Eagle's Nest* was within convenient walking distance from the railway station and the hotel. It was obviously suitable for travelers and locals alike. Most folks needed an invitation to just get inside.

The piano player filled the room with lively music. Sounds of multiple conversations added their own tones and rhythms to what some might have described as a raucous and cacophonous din. To Jim Link's ears it was symphonic.

Jim was New Orleans born and bred. The music, the crowd, the noise, and the opulence were all part of his life and the atmosphere of home. "Now this is more like it!" he exclaimed.

Tuck grinned and shook his head at Jim's enthusiasm. "I'll have a couple with ya, but then I'm goin' t' git sumthin' t' eat, git down t' the telegraph an' let Broome know we got 'er out safe. Then I'm gonna see what it feels like t' git a good night's sleep in a real bed."

Jim raised his eyebrows in mock surprise at Tuck's plans. "The trail don't seem t' have the same effect on everybody does it? I'm gonna have a couple with you, then a couple with her, an' a couple with her" Jim said, pointing out two of the saloon girls as he bantered with his partner. Pointing to a third, he spoke directly into Tuck's ear in secretive jest, "Then I'm gonna get bathed by that'n there, an' who knows whether Ole Jim'll git any sleep a'tall t'night?"

Tuck laughed and replied, "Ole Jim'll be lucky if he can afford drinks fer the first one, let alone gittin' a bath. Ya know they don't give nuthin' away doncha?"

"Why Tuck, she won't be givin' nuthin' away. When these ladies git t' know Ole Jimbo, they'll be fightin' over first rights t' me. It'll be them th't pays me!"

"If I wasn't so worn out, you terd bucket, I'd say this I gotta see. But, since I am, I wish ya luck."

Tuck and Jim sat down at a table and were instantly joined by two of the saloon girls. Jim ordered a round.

"Girls, don't confuse these two fer high rollers."

Tuck and Jim both looked up. It was Sheriff Hill.

"Sit down," Jim invited.

"Naw, I jus' stopped in here figurin' this was the closest place t' the hotel. I got a line on yer half-breed if ya wanna know."

"Who was he?" Tuck asked.

The sheriff looked around the room and shook his head.

"Not in here."

"Tell ya what Tuck. You go find out an' tell me later. These ladies an' me got serious business t'gether, don't we ladies?"

As Tuck stood to leave with the Sheriff he overheard one of the girls coo softly to Jim, "Serious business depends on if ya got serious money Honey." Tuck laughed, gave Jim an "I told you so" glance, and followed the sheriff outside.

"Oh ye of little faith!" Jim shouted after him.

Outside the night breeze was cool. In Tuck's opinion, city breezes lacked the crispness of the night air on a starlit plain or in a stand of trees beside a cold running stream. City breezes made you cold, but they weren't invigorating.

"Ya wanna walk over t' my office?"

"I'd jist's soon head on down t' the telegraph office. I need t' notify 'er husband that we got 'er out. Could we talk on the way?"

"Reckon so. This breed ya shot turns out t' be half Pawnee. Used t' scout fer the Army. One of about two hun'erd the Calv'ry used under the command of a Major North. My deputies say this breed stayed with the Pawnees mostly, but he's been called t' work fer the army a few times since the scouts got disbanded. Yer lucky ya seen 'im. He's backshot a few men. We know he did, but could never git no proof on 'im. So he ain't gonna be missed much 'round here."

"Have yer deputies got any idea a'tall why he came after us? Horses? The woman? What?"

"That's what I wanted t' talk to ya about. From what ya told me, he warn't after no horses."

"That's what I told Jim. They knew where the horses were."

The two men had been walking toward the railway station and were passing in front of the hotel.

"That deputy o' mine we got up there at her door ain't gonna last all night. He's been up since early this mornin'. Opened up the office an' the jail."

"Yeah, that's why I need t' git this telegraph off an' git back. Knowin' Jim he ain't gonna be much help t'night. Maybe not t'morra neither."

"I keep wonderin' what they was a doin' out

there on that freight road anyway. It ain't traveled that much, an' if they was trackin' ya then they prob'ly knew ya'd be out there. From what ya told me about that German, do ya think they worked fer him?"

"I've wondered a little 'bout that m'self," Tuck replied.

The two continued on in silence to the railway station.

Tuck sent a short message to an address in the nation's capital as Senator Broome had instructed: "BECKY SAFE STOP VOGEL RAN STOP NEED INSTRUCTIONS."

Back at the hotel he bid the sheriff good night and stopped at the desk. He still hadn't eaten. The clerk at the desk made arrangements with the kitchen and Tuck was served in his room. Tuck figured Senator Broome could afford it. After a hot meal and a bath Tuck longed for the comfort of his bed. However, he stepped across the hall and dismissed the deputy from his vigil at Becky's door and posted himself in the chair.

Becky had awakened at the sound of voices outside her door and just as Tuck had settled in the chair Becky opened the door a crack to peek out at him.

"I'm sorry Becky. We tried t' be quiet."

"I'm not sleepy anymore and I'm afraid by myself."

"Well ya don't need t' be. I'm right here."

"Have you had any sleep?"

"I'm alright."

"Come inside with me. You sleep. I'll be

awake."

Tuck squirmed. "Becky, I don't think that'd look very good."

She laughed, but not with humor. "After what I've been through I don't much care what it would look like. Get in here."

Tuck did as she commanded.

"If you don't mind sleeping with your clothes on just take off your boots and get some rest. I'll probably be awake the rest of the night."

Tuck hung his pistol belt over the end of the bed post, removed his boots, and laid back on the soft bed.

Becky pulled a rocking chair over to the window, pulled back the curtains, and sat watching the activity on the street below. After a few minutes of silence between them Becky spoke. "I want you to know that Klaus did not abduct me like Mason told you he did. I went willingly."

Tuck made no response.

Becky waited for his reply.

Tuck was snoring softly.

Becky sobbed as she stared out the window. The street was dark and only an occasional passerby disturbed the scene. She was afraid to go home. Why did Mason choose Tucker Spence to come after her? She was terribly confused. Although reality was more and more a part of her as each day passed, trying to sort things out sapped her of strength. Her mind refused to deal with reality for any extended periods.

She turned her gaze from the window to the man lying exhausted and asleep upon her bed. She had no doubt that Tucker Spence was foolishly enamored with her. For that very reason she had not spared him the details of her slavery to Klaus. She doubted any man would want her if he knew what she had been through with Klaus.

What would Mason do when he learned the whole truth? Mason was not a forgiving man. Becky knew him to be vain and prideful. The pride within Mason could at times be a great strength, but most often, his greatest weakness. How could he possibly face his family, his friends, and his constituents, if the details of her ordeal became public? Good deeds may never be widely acclaimed, but bad news has a life of its own that fights with a vengeance to become known. It would be insufferable enough for him had she been abducted, but, she had gone willingly. She knew Mason and she knew his pride. He could never forgive or forget what she had done.

Why should she go home she wondered? Even if he were willing to try, Mason would never be able to live with the truth. She had suffered so many things these past years at the hands of men that even the thought of her own husband expecting to be intimate with her filled her with revulsion. The last thing she wanted in her life now were obligations to a man.

She would always be grateful to Tuck and Jim for her rescue. There would always be a special place in her heart for them. However, the kind of feelings a man would want from her she was positive were dead within her.

She awoke with a start. Tuck was sitting on the

edge of the bed pulling on his boots.

"Did you spend the night in that chair?" he asked.

"Yes, but I'm fine. I must have dozed off. Its morning now I'll be okay. I'd like to freshen up and go down for breakfast."

"Yeah, sure... I'll be over in m' room across the hallway if ya want company." Tuck closed her door behind him.

He knocked on Jim's door. "You in there?"

"Yup," came Jim's muffled reply.

"You gonna go down an' eat?"

"Oh please!" Jim replied. The tone of his voice revealed the queasiness induced by his hangover.

At Becky's knock Tuck opened his door. She was in a fresh gingham dress of green and white, somewhat wrinkled from the packing, but clean and bright.

"Ya look mighty purty Becky."

She smiled ever so slightly and proceeded to lead the way down the hall to the stairway.

After a hearty breakfast of beefsteak and eggs, biscuits, and hot coffee, they sat gazing out the window as the morning sun's golden glare began to warm the day.

"He didn't feed ya reg'lar," Tuck observed.

"Sometimes, he didn't let me eat unless..." She stopped as she gazed down at herself, "I noticed this dress was a little loose fitting. I must have lost some weight."

Tuck resisted the urge to comment on how much weight she had lost in his estimation.

"Tucker, there's something I want you to know.

I'm afraid to go back."

Tuck looked at her with compassion and said, "Well, I can understand that some. What else did ya have in mind?"

"I don't know."

"You afraid o' Mason, or what?"

"Tucker, I was not abducted. I left Mason and went away with Klaus. I wish to God I'd never laid eyes on Klaus Vogel, but, that's what I did."

Tuck was speechless.

She waited, searching his face for his reaction.

When his response finally came it was delivered in disbelief and exasperation. "Well, that's not what he told me! Does he know that?"

"I don't know how he could help but know it. We didn't exactly sneak off."

"Fer cryin out loud!" Tuck vented through clenched teeth. He turned and glared out the window with his chin resting in his hand. The fingers of his hand squeezed the flesh of his face forming deep pockets in his jowls.

Becky remained silent.

"Ya know things'r startin' t' make sense in some ways an' makin' a whole lot less sense in others. I wonder what in the devil he thinks he's doin'," Tuck said.

"Do you see why I'm afraid to return to Kentucky? All of the time I was being used by Klaus... I was no more than a show horse... I longed to be home, wishing I'd never left." Tears welled up in her eyes as she gazed across the street her eyes avoiding Tuck's. "Since you and Jim came for me I've had time to get my thinking reorganized. I spent so long not really knowing what was real and what wasn't... No, now that I think about, I knew, but I was afraid to admit what was real."

Becky reached across the table and rested her hand on the back of Tuck's. She looked directly into his eyes through her tears and said, "How long ago was it? How did you get involved in all of this?"

A moment that Tuck would have moved heaven and earth to create was happening at that very instant, but he withdrew his hand and rested it in his lap. It was too late now. Some men might be able to ignore what Tuck knew had taken place with Becky. He could not–especially not now. When she had been a helpless victim he might have been able to deal with it. The thought of her with all those others, and knowing she left willingly, was more than he could handle.

Becky's eyes blazed with fierce pride as she withdrew her hand from the tabletop. "Do you see! And, you're not even my husband!" Becky had read Tuck's mind. "Don't think for one minute that Mason would ever forgive me for leaving him. When he finds out what I left him for and what I became he won't be man enough to deal with it either!" Her last remark was aimed in frustration to strike Tuck in an area she deemed him vulnerable.

Tuck didn't rise to the bait. The issue here wasn't his masculinity. The issue was the tarnished image of a damsel in distress.

The tension was thick when Jim finally arrived at the table. He pulled back a chair and said in a ragged voice, "Mornin'."

Jim was as ragged as his voice. His hair was

disheveled and his eyes were bloodshot. The odor of the previous night's libations was an unwelcome intrusion upon the breakfast atmosphere.

"Jim! D'ya mind sayin' yer good mornin's the other direction? These'r fresh flowers on the table an' I don't think they want 'em wilted this early in the day."

Jim leaned back in his chair, hooked his thumbs in his belt, and grinned at Tuck.

"And good gravy, don't grin out loud, we jist ate." Tuck was glad for the break in the mood and was intentionally playing to Jim's sense of humor waiting for the outburst that he knew was inevitable. Tuck badly needed a laugh, anything to replace the feelings he had at the moment.

Jim's mirth burst like a dam. He had such an infectious laugh that several of the other patrons turned and laughed at his outburst. Jim leaned toward Tuck and, breathing into his face, said, "H-o-o-o-o-w do ya like this?"

Tuck reeled backward pretending to nearly fall from his chair.

Becky was not amused.

"Ain't nothin' like a nasty drunk t' git yer day started, huh Becky?" Jim said, leering devilishly at her.

Becky turned her attention to Tuck. It was obvious she was not to be cajoled. "I don't find your friend amusing."

Jim raised an eyebrow in mild surprise and looked Becky up and down.

Tuck gave Becky a cold disapproving glance. "I don't give a hoot what ya find amusin' an' what ya don't. Jist don't fergit my unamusing friend saved yer butt when ya wuz out there bein' used... like a 'show horse' I believe ya said."

Becky stiffened at his remarks, stood up abruptly, turned, and stormed from the room.

"Well, I love you too," Jim called in the direction of her departure.

"Woman's startin' t' tick me off," Tuck said.

"What's 'er problem?" Jim asked.

"What ain't? Now she says she don't wanna go home t' her husband. Says she's scared of 'im."

The waitress approached their table and Jim ordered coffee.

"Why's she scared?"

"Well she dropped a load on me this mornin'. Told me she wasn't dragged off by the German. She went with him. Says her husband knows that... couldn't help but know it."

The waitress arrived with the coffee pouring Jim's cup and refilling Tuck's.

"Well, then what in the world 'r we doin' out here then?" Jim asked in bewilderment.

"Well, even after she told me that, I figgered it'd be reasonable, if he wanted 'er back he'd try t' git her. She says he ain't the fergivin' type an' she ain't sure she wants t' go home."

"Tuck, ya reckon he told us all that bull. cuz he was embarrassed fer us t' know the truth?"

"Could be... but I'll tell ya Jim, there just ain't nothin' right about this when I git t' thinkin' about it."

"We could always send 'im a telegram sayin' if he wants 'er, he can come git 'er," Jim suggested.

Tuck stirred the dark liquid in his cup as he stared out the window shaking his head in bewilderment.

When Becky reached her room, she slammed the door behind her and in anger threw herself across the bed.

CHAPTER 12

Mason Broome drummed his fingers on his desk as he sat staring at the two telegrams before him. Both bore him distressing news. The one on his left was from Tucker Spence stating that his wife was safe in Cheyenne, Vogel wasn't dead, and Spence needed instructions. The other was from Major Frank Pierce, an old college friend and accomplice, who, for the return of political favor, had agreed to arrange a favor for Mason. His telegram contained two words: "VOTE NO." It was a prearranged code meaning the attempted favor had been botched.

Mason seethed with anger and frustration. He had spent the morning considering his alternatives and reflecting upon the events that had led him to his dilemma. He had the same sinking sickness in the pit of his stomach that he'd felt the day he received a very disturbing letter from his overseer in Kentucky.

The letter revealed that Mrs. Broome had left

with Klaus Vogel giving no one instructions and leaving them without disposition to manage things. A wife's unfaithfulness was pain enough, but, to have his nose rubbed in the stigma of it by being disgraced in the eyes of his hired help was more than Mason could forgive. Moreover, if it were ever noised about, how could he ever face his peers in government? Becky and Vogel might just as well have publicly spit in his face. After all he had done for Klaus Vogel, how could he do this to him? They both had to be repaid.

Divorce was out of the question. It was too public, too messy, and the ruination of a political career. Divorce would surely expose the entire episode to public scrutiny.

His plan was to have the matter resolved in the western territories. Crime and lawlessness were a way of life on the frontier. If one met with violence in the west it was only what easterners would expect.

Mason's scheme to send a rescue mission and to concurrently and secretly arrange a bizarre incident was still sound even if the execution had been poor thus far.

If the scandal leaked he would be covered by the rescue arrangements and thought noble for attempting to rescue her. If all parties involved were dead no one would bother to try and sort out the facts.

Major Pierce was assigned to Fort Laramie and had been Mason's eyes and ears in the situation. Pierce knew of Vogel through contracts for horses purchased for the Army. Pierce had made a few discreet inquiries learning from the cowhands that Becky was for all practical purposes a prisoner.

Pierce made contact with a half-breed Pawnee scout who knew Vogel's foreman, a Mexican named Soto. It was from Soto that Pierce learned of the overnight visitations by Vogel's German acquaintances. Soto himself claimed to have been party to many of the events in the big house.

The thought of Becky with other men still sickened Mason in his soul. He seethed with anger and believed that it served her right for what she had done to him. But the humiliation of it for him was nearly more than he could bear. It ate at him every day. Their deeds must not go unpunished. Mason needed a plan and an executor. He had considered many avenues and many candidates. He had learned of Tucker Spence quite by accident through Becky's family, who had no knowledge of the real reason Becky left. Spence was considered to be somewhat of a crusader with a hard streak. By reputation, Tucker Spence was unflinching and unhesitating when a situation called for the use of a gun. There were consistent reports that Spence had no tolerance for anyone challenging him in any way at any time. It was evident that his family members were quite proud of his reputation for violence. They would never suspect that Broome fully intended to make use of that violence.

Mason considered Tucker Spence to be the candidate most likely to take immediate and deadly action against the swaggering and arrogant Klaus Vogel. The fact that Becky and Tucker Spence were childhood friends was almost more than he could hope for. He had a candidate with the skills, the temperament, and the motive for a rescue mission.

If Spence failed to kill Vogel, or Becky did not die in the rescue attempt, Major Pierce's half-breed would be waiting to finish the job.

But, Mason was not an experienced man on the trail and had severely underestimated the situation. Tucker Spence would not be an easy mark. Nor had Mason any idea that Spence's partner, Jim Link, was just as skilled as Spence and just as touchy, if not more so, and a seasoned trail veteran himself.

Mason took his pen and wrote replies to both telegrams. To Tucker Spence he sent: "STAY STOP COMING NEXT TRAIN." To Major Pierce he sent: "RECONSIDER," a code word to put into effect plan B.

"Mrs. Norton!" At his call Mason's secretary entered his office. "Please see that these telegrams are dispatched immediately and arrange for my transportation to the rail town of Cheyenne in the Wyoming territories please. I should expect to be gone for a period of at least three to four weeks. Please place on my desk anything requiring my attention prior to the end of those weeks."

"Why on earth are you going out there?" his secretary asked.

"Government business Mrs. Norton. Make the usual excuses for me and if inquiries are made you may say that I'm attending to urgent business, but I did not say where."

Mason walked the few blocks to his residence. The wind was from the north and brisk. Leaves of gold, orange, and rust blew across his path as he walked. Autumn throughout the Maryland area was spectacular.

When Mason opened the door to his suite of rooms at the hotel he was greeted by a strikingly beautiful woman. She had long raven hair, straight gleaming white teeth, made even more lustrous by the contrasting redness of her lips, a finely chiseled nose, high cheekbones, and a flawless butternut complexion. Mason had other reasons for making sure that Becky was taken out of the way.

Mandy was a Creole in her early twenties with an exquisite figure that filled her green satin dress. She flowed into Mason's arms and he kissed her passionately then held her at arms-length drinking in the sight of her.

"Mandy. You are beautiful. You're everything I've ever wanted."

Mandy returned his gaze evenly and replied with a touch of irony, "If that's so, when are you going to make me yours... publicly and permanently?"

"Soon Mandy, very soon."

Mandy was the reason why Broome had insisted that Becky remain in Kentucky to keep things going for him. It had all been just the way he wanted it; Mandy in the east to fill his passionate desires and Becky in Kentucky to keep his affairs back home in order. Becky and Klaus had ruined everything.

It wasn't that he didn't love Becky. But, he was in love with Mandy. However, Mandy was no longer content to be in the background and he could not bear to lose her. It was Mandy who had given him the support and courage he'd needed to bring things to a final close with Becky. Mandy understood politics and public scandal. When he confided in her that Becky had abandoned him for Klaus, she knew what he had to do and urged him to make it happen.

CHAPTER 13

Tuck stood in front of Becky's door with the telegram in his hand. It had taken him several hours since the messenger delivered it to decide to tell Becky. He was in a quandary where Becky was concerned. No matter what he said or did it was never the right thing. After the incident at breakfast two days before, he had avoided her. He initially thought he would ask Jim to relay the message to her, but, the way things had gone, Jim wasn't exactly in Becky's graces either.

Tuck knocked on her door.

When Becky opened the door, Tuck was overwhelmed by her beauty. Again, his defenses melted. Frustration was an understatement. Everything in him wanted her and yet everything in him was repulsed by what she had revealed to him.

She was regaining her color since she'd been eating regularly each day. Her face was no longer drawn and gaunt and her hair was shiny and clean.

She was a far cry from the underfed naked little prisoner he had found in that room at the ranch house.

"This came," he said, as he handed her the telegram from her husband.

She took the folded telegram from him without looking at it, smiled at Tuck, almost approvingly he thought, and invited him in. He glanced around her tidy room as he entered and noticed several tiny bottles on her dresser. She had at least ventured out to buy some personal things. Tuck found a woman's perfume usually a bit overwhelming. The whores in the saloons must bathe in it he thought. In Becky's case however, her subtle fragrance was spellbinding.

Becky seemed to be in a surprisingly good mood this morning as she took him by the arm and escorted him to the rocking chair next to her bed. When he was seated, she sat on the edge of the bed and read the telegram.

"When will he be here?" she asked, with a touch of dread in her voice.

"The depot agent said by the end of the week... Saturday, if he got on the train the day the telegram was sent out," he replied.

"Tucker," she began, with a disarming sweetness in her voice, "would you do me a favor? I know you've been through a lot for me and a lot since you've been with me." She paused to judge his reaction.

Tuck was attentive but his face showed no trace of reaction. *Lady, you don't know the half of it,* he thought to himself.

She continued, "I know this is going to sound crazy, but I want you to take me back to the ranch."

"To Vogel's?" he blurted.

"Yes" she responded stiffly. "There are things there that I paid plenty for!" Becky checked her anger and continued more calmly, "And, if Mason wants me he can come and get me on my terms, not his."

Tuck shook his head in disbelief. *Just when you think you've heard it all,* he mused to himself. "Now Becky, we come a long way t' git ya here. We've sold the rig an…"

"I checked yesterday, the livery hasn't sold the carriage or the team yet and the man said he'd sell them back to us if we'd pay for the provender." Her eyes were alive and sparkled as she spoke. "Tuck, can't you see. For me it's like being thrown from a horse, you've got to get back up and ride, and I need to go back to the place where I lost control of my life and take control of it again."

Well now, he thought. *Ain't that something?* What if Vogel had gone back to his ranch thinking they had just rode away without regard for him? That would suit Tuck just fine because Vogel was unfinished business that would eventually be completed.

She studied his face for a few moments and then began again. "I know Mason. I'm married to him. I'm not sure it could ever work for us. There had to be something wrong or I wouldn't have gone in the first place. Oh, yes, I was stupid, and believe me, I paid for my stupidity. But, I don't believe I want Mason back in my life. I can't believe he would really want me back in his. And, I'm very sure that if I go back with him my life will be Hell... a different kind than with Klaus, but Mason will make me pay every day. That's his nature." She waited, surveying Tuck's face again for signs of comprehension and compassion.

Tuck had played many poker games and faced many situations, long ago learning not to let his face reveal his thoughts to anyone.

"The man's comin' out here t' git ya. What're ya gonna do about that?"

"We'll leave word with the hotel, or the sheriff, where we've gone... and if he wants me he can come after me. I'm not playing a game Tuck. If I'm going to face him I want it to be on level ground."

Tuck could understand that. Any time you faced someone you needed to pick the time and place if you could. However, he couldn't see what difference it made in this case.

"Have you thought about what happens if Vogel is back at his ranch? Besides, I don't think Jim'll go for it."

"Unless I'm wrong, he'll go. But, if he doesn't, you and I can go. And, as for Vogel, I'd give a lot to be there when he had to face someone he couldn't bully. I want him dead!"

Tuck made no reply to her. As far as he was concerned getting back on the trail was a very great idea. He hated towns. But, going back to Vogel's ranch immediately wasn't exactly what he had in mind. Besides, he had no intention of leaving his partner so he could accompany a woman, who thus far saw no more value in him than a convenient escort, on a journey designed to give her some imagined advantage in patching things up with her husband. "I'll have t' think about this awhile," he said shaking his head. As he stood to leave Becky rose from the bedside and placed her hand on his arm.

"Please Tucker, I know it's an awful lot to ask, but, I need to go back there."

"Like I said, I'll have t' think about it. I'll talk t' Jim."

He found Jim at the saloon, which had only been open about an hour.

"My kinda place," Jim said grinning.

Tuck gazed at him in mock disbelief.

"You'da been proud o' me las' night Tuck. I had three of 'em. Emptied m' gun so many times the last shot was jist dust... well you know me, I knew better than t' go fer blood!" Jim laughed uproariously.

Tuck shook his head this time in genuine amazement, then replied, "So, what yer tellin' me is, ya had one old poxed up whore and ya was so drunk ya couldn't do a thing."

Jim erupted with laughter again concluding with, "Yeah right!"

"Well..." Tuck began, "I talked t' the crazy woman t'day. You ain't gonna believe what she wants t' do."

"She wants t' go back t' the ranch," Jim said matter-of-factly.

"How did you know?" Tuck asked in utter surprise.

"She asked me t' take 'er yesterday evenin'...

came t' my room big as ya please. Well, I was on m' way out, told 'er I'd talk t' ya about it, but I see she already did."

Tuck could feel his neck redden and sensed the heat creeping into his face.

"Did she ask ya t' take 'er an' leave me out of it?"

Jim shifted uncomfortably in his chair. "Yeah, she did, but you know how much chance there is o' that. I was gonna talk to ya about it t'day but I wasn't gonna mention that. I s'pose she told ya that."

"No, she didn't. She asked me t' take 'er an' leave you out... I figgered she'd probably tried t' play us off against one another." Tuck ordered a whiskey.

"Little early in the day fer you ain't it?" Jim inquired impishly.

"Used t' be," Tuck replied.

"Well," Jim exclaimed, "ya know what I think? If she wants 'er self back out there, let's take 'er. We'll leave a message fer ole what's his name, an' then let's me an' you shuck ourselves o' this mess. If her husband arrives first, he can deal with Vogel. If Vogel is there, or shows up, we'll give him greetings from both Becky and Nate."

Jim downed the remainder of his drink and reordered. The bartender refilled Jim's glass and poured one for Tuck. *If it were only that simple,* Tuck thought.

Unfortunately, there was no way that Tucker Spence could mentally shuck himself of Becky. *There may come a time, when for my own good, I'll have to cut my losses though,* he thought. Turning to

Jim he said, "Let's think about it fer awhile. I got a telegram early this mornin' from Broome. He'll be here sometime this weekend more'n likely."

"She knew about that an' still wanted t' go?" Jim asked.

"Yep, she's got some notion that when they meet it needs t' be on her terms."

"Yeah, but why all the way back there?"

Tuck looked at Jim incredulously and said, "I hope you don't expect me t' answer that."

That evening Tuck joined Becky in the hotel dining room. "It's purty obvious you don't care which one of us goes or stays... Jim's willin' t' go back t' the ranch if that's what ya want. I can't say I think it's right or wrong, but fer me bein' on the trail beats bein' in town. We kin leave in the mornin' if ya want. I'll leave word with the sheriff. He'll notify yer husband."

"That's what I want," she replied. "I gave the livery man back the money for the team and the carriage today. Can you pay for the keep of the horses?"

Tuck looked at Becky with mild surprise. "Purty sure o' yerself ain't ya?" Tuck shook his head in disbelief and said, "I'll go take care of it now and we'll head out in the morning. I gotta get some supplies before the general store closes."

Tuck stopped by the store to purchase supplies and made arrangements to pick them up early the following morning. He walked down the street to the livery and settled the account for provender. The keeper promised to have the horses rigged at first light.

Next, Tuck stopped by to tell the sheriff of the change in plans. When questioned by the sheriff, Tuck could only reply that he was just passing on the message not trying to explain it. Finally, he headed for the saloon where he was sure to find Jim.

Becky sat in her hotel room watching out the window as Tucker Spence walked past on his way to the saloon. She had to admit that Tucker was an attractive man and, for the briefest moment, wondered how differently her life might have been if she had been the wife of this man from Missouri.

Becky had no way of knowing the sinister plans that Mason Broome had for her, but something inside her cried caution. That same voice had called out to her when she was leaving with Klaus Vogel and she had ignored it. This time she was paying close attention.

In Becky's mind, the ranch and the house were not the evil that she had escaped; Klaus was. She knew Klaus had paid cash for the ranch. Therefore, if he were dead, the likelihood of anyone doubting her claim to the ranch would be remote. She was also confident that none of his close relatives would be coming to the territories from Germany to claim it. Especially when they learned that he'd met his end for the hanging of an innocent boy and the abuse of a woman. In the end, she would rather be master of her own fate on that remote ranch than return to Kentucky and be in subjection to a man who could never forgive her for her infidelity. She was not about to become another man's slave, physically or emotionally. Husband or not, she had decided she was not returning to Kentucky.

It had been a mistake to run away with Klaus. It would be a mistake to return to Kentucky with Mason and do penance the remainder of her life. If Mason came after her she would simply face him with the facts. He could divorce her if he chose, or, simply go home and forget her.

She didn't love Mason anymore. In her heart she still couldn't forgive him for failing to come after her, even if she had brought her troubles upon herself. She knew that wasn't rational, but, that was how she felt. Mason didn't even care enough about her to accompany the men he sent.

When Tuck entered the saloon, he saw Jim seated with two of the bar girls. He sat in an empty chair at Jim's table. One of the girls was pressuring Jim to buy her another drink while the other sat gazing disinterestedly across the room.

"Good t' see ya Tuck. As you kin see, I got a friend for ya," Jim said.

The girl who had been staring across the room came to life at Tuck's arrival. She slipped her arm through his and pulled her chair closer to Tuck's. "How 'bout a drink Honey," she whispered in his ear as she twirled her finger in the hair at the nape of his neck.

The pungent aroma of too much perfume, in an unsuccessful attempt to cover the odor of an unwashed body, rose offensively in Tuck's nostrils. He looked at the girl's face. It was caked with powder and rouge and her smile revealed two unsightly rows of rotted teeth. "No thanks, think I'll pass," he replied.

"Well then!" she retorted saucily. The girl rose without further comment and walked to a table where four new arrivals were just being seated.

Seeing the expression on Tuck's face, Jim blurted out, in feigned innocence, "What?"

CHAPTER 14

Major Frank Pierce had donned civilian clothing, to be less conspicuous, while he accompanied the three men he had chosen to carry out the alternate assignment Mason Broome had given him. He intended to take the measure of the two men seated at the table across the saloon from him before proceeding with his plan. Pierce had obviously underestimated them last time. This time he would personally direct the situation.

Pierce was sorry he had ever become involved in this sordid mess. He had met Becky at an affair in Philadelphia when she and Mason were first married. He remembered her as being radiantly beautiful. It was a shame to put such beauty to an end. Personal debts had forced Major Pierce to accept Mason Broome's proposal. Pierce not only owed Broome money, he owed him for several important, and if ever revealed, career ruining favors. Broome had offered to wipe the slate clean if Pierce would perform this one final task for him.

Pierce wasn't squeamish about killing, not even killing for hire. In his mind, most of the "riddances," as he called them, were a service to mankind. Killing Becky Broome didn't fit in that category. A distasteful task indeed, but made far more distasteful to him because it couldn't be done quickly and cleanly. In order to mask his and Mason's involvement it was essential that Becky be abducted. Her abduction had to be done in a manner that would lead others to believe that Vogel was behind it. It must appear to be another case of a woman being raped and murdered by frontier cutthroats. The men Pierce were using were being paid to keep their mouths shut. Part of their price was that they could do as they pleased with the woman.

As Pierce sat at a table across the saloon from Tuck and Jim he tried to size them up. Killing Soto at the ranch and the half-breed on the trail had certainly enhanced his respect for the two.

The three men Pierce had with him were more expensive than the half-breed had been. However, Pierce had used all three in the past and he knew their worth.

Sonny Spears was the youngest of the three and the wildest. He was an unpredictable hothead with a reputation for being fast on the draw and a penchant for showing off.

Whitey Cline was a huge and extremely powerful man. He had earned a reputation with his fists. Cline carried a sidearm but much preferred the pleasure of breaking another man's body with his bare hands.

Al Simmons, nicknamed "Weasel," was a rustler, a horse thief, a backstabber, and a back-shooter. In Pierce's view, Simmons was one of the most treacherous, vile, and repulsive characters he'd ever met. Those were sterling qualifications for what Pierce had in mind.

The bar girl seated on Whitey Cline's lap was becoming an irritant as she whined her solicitations for a drink.

"Get rid of her," Pierce said to Cline.

Whitey picked the girl up by the waist and stood her on the floor. "We got business," he said, and turned back to the table. The girl stormed off without looking back.

"One thing I wanna git clear," Simmons said, peering at the others with his close set squinty eyes, "I git first crack at the woman... we all agreed t' that?"

Pierce thought that "Ratface" would have been a more appropriate nickname for the despicable Simmons. There was no reply from the others and Simmons seemed satisfied that a lack of response was a sign of agreement.

"Remember, I cannot be implicated in this in any way. Before you start anything, make sure I have time to get to the Sheriff's office. I have to have an ironclad alibi," Pierce instructed.

"Well, here's the way I see it. Simmons and Cline'll go git the woman, an' I'll keep these two entertained," Spears said contemptuously, as he nodded in the direction of Tuck and Jim.

"Do you think that's the best plan," Pierce

asked, "sending two of you against one woman and one of you against the two bounty hunters?"

"Think ya kin handle 'em Spears?" Cline challenged with a laugh.

"Easy" Spears replied, grinning at Cline.

"Seeing as how it's my money, we'll do it my way," Pierce ordered. "Simmons and Spears will take these two and Cline'll get the woman."

"I s'pose that'd be smarter," Simmons ventured, "but remember Whitey, I git 'er first. An' Spears, if you wanna take 'em both I'll back ya up."

"Yeah, I know you do yer best work in the back Weasel," Spears chided.

Simmons hated his nickname but had long ago learned not to make it an issue with anyone he couldn't overpower.

"Maybe we ought to try and separate them," Pierce suggested.

Spears bristled, interpreting Pierce's caution as doubting his abilities. "These two? We got 'em both together an' that's the best time t' git it done with," he argued.

Pierce acquiesced and rose to leave.

"Give me twenty minutes to get down to the sheriff's office so I don't look like I just walked in thirty seconds the whole thing breaks loose. Cline'll take the woman when he hears the ruckus start."

Cline rose and followed Pierce out of the saloon.

Pierce crossed the street and Cline strolled casually toward the hotel.

Pierce and Sheriff Hill were previously acquainted and within a few minutes of Pierce's arrival at Hill's office they were engaged in bringing each other up to date on events occurring since their last meeting.

In the meantime, Cline took his place in the room Pierce had rented for him just across the hall from Becky. Cline had established that Becky was in her room by knocking on her door. When she answered it he apologized stating he thought it was the room of a friend and departed immediately.

After seeing Becky, Cline was positive that Weasel was not going to be first–maybe not at all.

Back in the saloon, Spears and Simmons were working their nerve up with liquor.

"What're we gonna do if they leave b'fore we've gived Pierce 'nuff time?" Simmons asked.

"We'll follow 'em out an' take 'em in the street," Spears replied.

Years of experience had not been wasted on Tuck or Jim. They made it their business to observe everything around them without being obvious about it.

"Have ya noticed how many times them ole boys over there have looked our way since you was unkind t' that little lady that I had reserved just fer you? I can't imagine why you weren't interested in her."

"Yeah, I have. I also noticed she didn't stay long enough fer their interest in us t' be any concern over her, unless they're watchin' t' see if I got struck blind 'r the little witch turned me into a toad," Tuck replied. "Oh good grief Jim, she didn't did she?"

"Well, yeah, but a handsome toad,"   Jim

answered.

"You ever see 'em b'fore?" Jim asked without looking in the direction of the men he was referring to.

"Nope. Ain't never seen the two that left neither."

"Well, I reckon we're gonna find out," Jim said as the two men they were discussing rose and started walking toward them.

When Spears and Simmons arrived at the table where Tuck and Jim were seated they stood side by side.

"Mind if we join ya? Mebbe play some cards?" Spears began.

Jim, who under ordinary circumstances was quite gregarious, replied tersely, "We ain't real fond o' playin' cards."

Spears pressed the point. "Jist bein' neighborly... mebbe you ain't too fond o' bein' neighborly neither," he replied.

"No, we ain't particular big on neighbors. You got somethin' in yer craw? Or, are you just too dumb to know when someone don't like you?" Tuck interjected.

Simmons moved cautiously away from Spears. He hated this kind of encounter. It was too risky. He preferred to lie in wait and let them have it before they knew what hit them.

Things weren't exactly going the way Spears had hoped they would either. These two were on the prod. Spears was much more accustomed to making his play by catching men off guard, before they became fully aware of his intentions. However, he couldn't back down now. He had to play it as it happened.

"You two're kinda pushy with yer mouths ain't ya? That always makes me wanna see if a man's got anything t' back up a pushy mouth," Spears retorted.

Jim made the first reply, "Why don't you jist go do what the other little boys 'r doin b'fore ya git too carried away with yerself. You got some kinda problem?"

"I think you got a problem, you reckon you kin talk down t' whoever ya want without no fear o' gittin' yer mouth shut." Spears spat the words venomously and loudly at the two.

Jim scooted back in his chair a little and turned toward Simmons while Tuck remained face to face with Spears.

Jim spoke to Simmons, "Let's see, yer friend here's a real fast draw right?"

"Purty fast," Simmons replied. His eyes were even narrower under stress and his mouth twitched nervously.

Without averting his eyes from Simmons, Jim said to Spears, "Well now son, let me ask ya one question... after ya draw real fast, how many shots do ya need t' do the job?" Without waiting for Spears to reply he continued, "Cuz ya see boy, it ain't how fast yer draw is, it's how fast yer kill is."

Jim and Tuck had faced many men who could clear leather faster than either of them. The difference was that neither Tuck nor Jim hesitated when the time came. Most men had to work up their nerve. They didn't. It was simple logic. When a situation could not be averted they moved first.

"Well why don't we jist step outside an' see?" Spears challenged.

"Let me git this straight. You want us t' git up an' go outside cuz we didn't wanna play cards with ya, is that it?" Tuck asked the question in a voice loud enough to get the attention of witnesses. People began getting up from their chairs immediately and moving out of the path of the foursome.

Spears misread Tuck's question as a plea for calm. He became more aggressive and shouted at Tuck, "No that ain't it! You two terd whackers shot yer mouths off an I'm gonna close 'em fer ya!" His face reddened as he worked his temper up. "That kinda crap'll git ya killed where I come from!"

Jim laughed. "Sounds like ya mean t' take us both. What's yer handsome friend gonna do?" Jim asked, having never taken his eyes off Simmons.

"He normally goes an' gits the undertaker fer me," Spears said coldly, regaining some composure, "an' you git up an' come outside boy an' I'll give ya some lead t' laugh about."

By this time, the confrontation had arrested the attention of everyone in the bar. The bar girls and the rest of the patrons were hastily moving out of the line of fire.

"Let's do it," Tuck said calmly. He and Jim rose together. The moment they were sufficiently clear of the table they drew. Their two colts roared simultaneously. Simmons and Spears fell backwards.

Spears landed on his back with his gun partially

out of the holster. He was shot in the heart and probably dead when he hit the floor. Simmons' hand never made it to the grip of his sidearm. He was also shot in the middle of the chest. He lived just long enough to wheeze, "Shudna faced 'em... I knew it."

When Whitey Cline heard the gunfire he hesitated. It sounded like only one shot had been fired. His instructions were to act when he heard gunfire, but he had expected more than one shot. He was supposed to break into Becky's room, render her helpless, and carry her down the back stairs of the hotel where his horse was tied and waiting. He decided it must be the time to do it.

Cline crossed the hall to Becky's room, put his shoulder to the door and crashed through, easily breaking the bolt loose from the door casing.

Becky screamed as Cline burst into her room and a shot rang out. Cline dove toward the bed where the frightened Becky sat propped against the headboard with her knees drawn almost to her chin. Another shot rang out and Cline was on top of her. She screamed again.

Downstairs at the desk the night clerk jumped out of his chair behind the desk exclaiming, "What the...?" He grabbed a sawed off shotgun from under the desk and proceeded cautiously up the stairs. His blood ran cold as he heard Becky screaming continually now.

When he reached the top of the stairs he saw no one in the hall. Very carefully, he peered through the door of the screaming woman's room to quickly assess the situation with the shotgun at the ready.

He wasn't a particularly brave man but Becky's incessant and frantic screams had compelled him to act.

What he saw frightened him but he heard himself shouting, "Git offa her ya mongrel!" He stepped through the door with the shotgun leveled at the giant hulk of a man who lay atop the screaming woman. "Git offa her 'r I'm gonna shoot ya square in the behind!"

Becky's screaming stopped at the sound of the clerk's voice and he could hear her choking and sobbing beneath the weight of her attacker.

The man did not move. The confused clerk took a tentative step toward Cline, still lying on top of Becky. His shotgun was still at the ready. There were two bloody holes in the man's back and blood was spreading rapidly on the sheets. It appeared to be pouring from Becky's side.

The clerk was horrified. He reached out and grabbed Cline by the back of his shirt and yanked. Cline rolled off Becky and on to the floor. It was then that the clerk could see Becky clutching a large pistol in both hands. Her hands, arms, the pistol, and the front of her dress, were all covered with blood.

The front of Cline's shirt was soaked with blood. His eyes were wide open and fixed in a sightless stare. "Girl, are ye stabbed?" the clerk asked Becky seeing no weapon other than hers. She had tears streaming down her face and she was biting her bottom lip as she shook her head no.

The clerk stepped to the window, raised it, and shouted to the crowd gathering on the street at the front of the hotel, "Somebody git the sheriff an' the doctor up here, fast!"

Sheriff Hill had heard the shots from the saloon and had run out the door of his office, mounted his horse, and began racing toward the saloon. Halfway down the street he heard two shots ring out in succession from the direction of the hotel. He had reined his horse to a stop in the middle of the street.

Now what is going on? He thought to himself. *It must be the bank! They're trying to draw us off in two directions.* He then spurred his horse toward the bank.

When Major Frank Pierce heard what he also assumed was a single shot, fear gripped him. He had the sinking feeling that something had gone wrong. When he heard two shots from the hotel he knew something was crazy. He also ran from the sheriff's office, mounted his horse, and rode down the alley between the sheriff's office and the building next door. Checking to make sure he wouldn't be seen, he rode away towards open country.

Everything at the bank had seemed normal to Sheriff Hill and he wheeled his horse toward the hotel. A gunshot from the saloon wasn't all that unusual, but gunshots from the hotel were.

The sheriff took the hotel stairs two at a time. There were already several men in the hall outside Becky's room.

"Thank God yer here sheriff," the clerk blurted when he saw Hill. "This woman's kilt a man here. When I got here he was on top o' her... an' he'd busted the door in. I thought she was stabbed 'r shot, but she's okay I guess."

As Sheriff Hill surveyed the grisly scene he knew that two attempts on the same woman just couldn't be coincidence.

Within minutes one of his deputies arrived. "I checked out the saloon Sheriff! Two dumb fools tried callin' them bounty hunters out and got themselves killed!"

"What in tarnation is goin' on here?" Sheriff Hill asked to no one in particular.

Later that night, with Becky safely installed in a different room, and a deputy on guard, Tuck, Jim, and Sheriff Hill reviewed the strange events.

Jim was cleaning the dried blood from the revolver that Becky had used to defend herself against Cline.

"She said she pulled that outa Jim's pack down at the stable the other day when she was inquirin' about the team. It's the gun Jim took off that half-breed." Tuck explained to Hill. "Becky says she's felt all along that she needed protection and figured she couldn't count on us." Tuck felt mildly embarrassed as he related Becky's views to the sheriff.

Jim laughed. "Looks like she was right!" he observed and laughed again. "I'd fergot all about that ole pistol. It's a good thing she hadn't. She said that Cline'd knocked on 'er door earlier sayin' he was lookin' fer a friend. Becky said the way he looked at 'er she suspected that she was the friend he had in mind... she was scared t' go t' sleep an' she'd been sittin' on the bed with the gun 'tween 'er knees facin' the door."

Sheriff Hill scratched his head and then after pondering a bit said, "The thing that still worries me is, you said they was four of 'em in the saloon an' we've only accounted fer three. The other one is loose out there somewhere."

"Yeah, that's a fact. The two dumb butts down at the saloon only had one thing in mind, an' that was t' git us," Jim said, referring to Spears and Simmons. "Ya seldom see anybody that anxious t' git killed."

"An' it looks like the plan was fer the third one t' kill Becky once the shootin' started," the Sheriff ventured as he walked to the door of his office and peered into the night. "But what was the fourth one up to? Yer sure you never saw him b'fore?"

Tuck and Jim both shook their heads no. None of them suspected what Becky's real fate would have been if the abduction attempt had been successful.

"Well, there's only two people I kin figger wants 'er dead, it's gotta be like she says, her husband, or that German," Tuck offered.

"I agree," Jim said, "only thing is, how we gonna figure out which one it is? An' why the devil would her husband send us t' git 'er if all he wanted was t' have 'er killed? He coulda had that done without this much trouble."

Sheriff Hill turned and said, "Well if it's him, he's tried twice. I think he underestimated you two. If it's Vogel, I ain't got no idea why he'd go t' all the trouble. One side o' me want's t' decide it's him an' the other side says it jis' don't make sense."

Tuck was leaning forward in his chair with his

elbows resting on his knees and his hands clasped together. He stared vacantly at the floor and without looking up said, "Mebbe that's it... a bunch o' smoke that don't make no sense so he'd come out clean."

The Sheriff and Jim looked at each other and shook their heads in agreement that Tuck's observation was a possibility.

"She still wants t' go t' the ranch in the morning," Jim stated flatly.

"Looks like a better plan all the time," was Tuck's reply. "You take 'er. I'm gonna stay here an' wait on Broome. Him and me's got a few things t' discuss... If he ain't involved in this, 'r I can't prove it, I'll bring 'im out. If he is I'll try t' git 'im t' tip his hand."

"Oh, sure, you stay here with the nice warm whores an' send me out t' be with the crazy woman," Jim said in disbelief.

"Well, the facts are, Broome don't know you, an' she don't like me," Tuck argued.

Jim couldn't rebut the first point but the second point didn't count because Jim knew she didn't like him any better.

The Sheriff broke in, "Years ago, if any strangers came in t' town people noticed. Nowadays, there's so many people movin' around, with strangers comin' through, people don't pay attention. I'll ask around t' see if anyone seen the four ride in, or kin describe the fourth man."

"We prob'ly got as good a look at 'im as anyone," Tuck declared.

Tuck and Jim collaborated to give Sheriff Hill a description of the fourth man with as much detail as they could remember. Their description matched the one he'd received from his deputy who had interrogated the saloon girls. Sheriff Hill was sure the deputy's details were describing Major Frank Pierce, and now Tuck and Jim's description confirmed it. He said nothing to them about his conclusion.

Early the next morning, Tuck had the carriage, loaded with supplies, sitting in front of the hotel. The three of them ate breakfast together before Jim and Becky began the long trek back to the ranch south of Crayt.

The morning was cool. The days were becoming crisper and the nights were cold as what appeared to be an early winter threatened to strengthen its grasp on the area.

"I bought extra blankets an' packed 'em in the back," Tuck said.

"Well, I think we'll be fine with what we got in the buggy an' what I'm bringin' on Dusty," Jim said referring to the dappled gray gelding that had been his mount for several years and now served as his packhorse.

"How come ya ain't named that sorrel mare yet?" Tuck asked.

"Why? You ain't never named a horse that I know of." Looking at Becky Jim continued, "Tuck jist calls his horse *horse*. We had a dog once that he jist called *dog*." Returning his attention to Tuck he said, "A mare's different than a gelding. In my opinion a gelding sorta loses his personality after they fix him. Good strong mount but not much personality. You kin name 'em purty easy. Now a mare, she's different, kinda sensitive... sometimes their mean an' sassy... an' this one I'm still tryin' t' figger out. She's sassy but runs the trail like an arrow."

Becky shifted impatiently in her chair.

Jim read her signal and said, "Yeah, speakin' of the trail, we better git on down it."

Becky rose immediately and started for the door.

Tuck lagged behind intentionally and caught Jim by the arm.

"Watch yerself out there. If you think Vogel's at the ranch, wait for me. It won't take me long to catch up."

"I will," Jim said. "Ya know if we wait too long out here we're gonna end up havin' t' wade through snow 'r take the train back. I'd appreciate it if ya didn't mess around with Broome too long. You know how these things are... once they see each other again it could all be different. We might never be able t' prove anything even if it is him."

Tuck had to agree with Jim, especially where Becky was concerned. He slapped Jim on the back and said, "I hear ya."

Becky was already in the seat when the two men stepped out on the hotel porch.

Jim tied his horses to the back of the carriage, mounted the seat, snapped the reins, and he and Becky were off. Jim waved without looking back. Becky made no noticeable move.

Tuck shook his head. "What a mess," he said aloud, as he watched the carriage roll out of town.

CHAPTER 15

A telegram had been delivered to Mason Broome at the last station stating: "SECOND VOTE NO STOP NO THIRD BALLOT." Major Frank Pierce was relating his failed second attempt and that he had no intention of making another. Broome wadded up the telegram in his fist. Something inside him urged him to quit before he became inextricably embroiled in what was rapidly appearing to be a ruinous situation. So far it had all the earmarks of a very bad plan. Bitterness welled up within him at each occasion of caution and he doggedly determined to carry on regardless of the cost.

It was obvious now however, that if he were to exact his revenge upon Becky, he would have to do it himself. It was an unsettling thought for him. He was not accustomed to being directly involved in violence preferring instead to make use of those more suited to it.

As Mason traveled ever closer, unaware that Becky was now on her way back to the ranch, his uneasiness increased. Nothing had gone right. Would he be able to mask his anger long enough to effect another plan once he stood face to face with her? Still, it was too late to turn aside from the course he had set for himself. If he were to allow Becky's return to Kentucky there were simply too many questions and the answers were more than he could bear. He refused the thought of such humiliation.

Mason stared out the window at the countryside. It seemed stark and barren to him. The occasional view of a rocky plateau was the only break in what he considered wide-open monotony. The rhythmic sounds of the wheels were hypnotic as the train rolled across the remaining miles to Cheyenne.

It was late evening when Mason stepped down from the passenger car at the station in Cheyenne. A young boy called out to the passengers gathering on the platform, "Mr. Broome? Mr. Mason Broome?" Mason acknowledged the call and the messenger informed him that he'd been tasked to escort him to the sheriff's office upon his arrival. Mason's blood ran cold for a moment. Had Pierce revealed to the law Mason's part in the attempts on Becky's life? He was the only one who could have. Why wasn't Spence there to meet him? He feared something was seriously wrong.

Another voice called his name. Mason turned and recognized Tucker Spence striding toward him.

"I've got a hotel room reserved for ya. The

hotel's within easy walkin' distance... we kin git yer bags an' git ya settled in. I 'spect yer wore out,"

Tuck spoke as warmly as he could manage considering his suspicions. Tuck flipped the messenger a coin and said, "I'll see that he gits to the Sheriff son."

Tuck's demeanor calmed Mason considerably. Surely if there were any suggestion of impropriety on his part the Sheriff himself would have confronted him.

"Good. By the way, the Sheriff, do you have any idea what he might want?" Mason asked innocently.

"Well we've had a little problem since we been here, I'll tell ya 'bout it on the way."

Mason had no trouble appearing to be appalled, amazed, and dismayed, by the story Tuck related to him. He actually was appalled, at the ineptness demonstrated by Pierce in the two attempts on Becky's life. He was certainly amazed to hear that Becky had actually killed one of her attackers, and he was truly dismayed that Becky had returned to the ranch.

All of his rehearsals concerning what to say and what to do upon their first encounter had been for naught. She wasn't even here.

"What if Vogel is still there? I want to leave for the ranch first thing tomorrow," Mason said to Tuck.

"I thought maybe you'd want t' rest up here fer at least a day," Tuck replied.

"No, I've rested quite enough," Mason joked, patting his backside. "I'll get a good night's sleep and then I'll be ready to ride in the morning."

Tuck thought there were still many unresolved issues he intended to address, but in the days on the trail he would deal with them. He wondered what he would have done if he were in Mason's shoes and Becky had run off with another man. Loving a woman could make a man crazy enough to do things a sane man wouldn't.

Mason was a skilled politician and prided himself on being able to interpret the mood of his listeners. He sensed that Tuck was uncomfortable with him and that he wanted to say something but was keeping himself continually in check.

Mason considered it essential to get Tuck and Jim out of the way if he were to succeed, but how? He was no match for them in a head to head confrontation. He hoped to convince them that everything was fine and when they moved on he and Becky would be alone. He knew he was going to have to convince Becky as well.

After all, from Mason's point of view, the attempts on Becky's life had been unsuccessful, and other than being extremely frightened, she hadn't really been harmed. As long as Pierce remained silent no one could prove anything. Even if Mason himself were a suspect, by his reasoning, he really wasn't guilty of anything yet.

He decided to make an attempt to win the confidence of Tucker Spence. "I suppose by now you have realized that some of the things I told you prior to sending you out here were not entirely true. There were reasons for that and I will be glad to explain them on the way to the ranch," Mason declared.

Tuck, caught off guard by Mason's admission, didn't say anything for a moment but stared straight into Mason's eyes. Mason did not look away and Tuck saw no sign of fear or nervousness.

Politics had long ago taught Mason Broome that skillful lying was a needful art and an everyday part of the business. Any conscience he might have had was seared long ago. After all, what he had just told Tuck was nearly the truth. Mason had misled Tuck prior to sending him on his mission. Mason did fully intend to give Tuck reasons for that, even if the reasons were to be more lies.

"Well I better get some things t'gether. Ain't no way t' buy a decent ridin' horse here. Army buys 'em up as soon as any decent horses come up fer sale. I'll ride my roan, he's prob'ly had his feelin's hurt carryin' pack. You kin ride the buckskin your money bought me. I can buy a decent packhorse at the liv'ry," Tuck offered.

"I presume you still have sufficient funds? Purchase the best saddle you can please. I don't ride as much as I used to."

After checking Mason into the hotel, Tuck escorted him to the sheriff's office and introduced him to Sheriff Hill. Excusing himself Tuck set about making preparations for the trail.

Sheriff Hill recounted to Mason many of the same details that Tuck had covered. When he finished his account he paused to see if Mason had any questions or comments.

"Well, I can see she has had quite a time of it. She was exceedingly fortunate I think to be in the company of the men I selected. It has to be that maniac Klaus Vogel who is behind all of this," Mason stated in as convincing a manner as he could.

Sheriff Hill was not taken in. He prided himself in knowing when a man was lying and when he was telling the truth. He was sure that Broome was a phony and decided to press for proof. "How long have ya known Major Frank Pierce?" Hill asked matter-of-factly.

Mason Broome was no amateur either. He and Pierce had previously agreed to disavow knowing each other if the time ever came that someone tried to make a connection. Of course it could be proved that they did know each other, but Mason was confident, not by any frontier lawman's efforts. "Who?" Mason asked innocently.

"Major Frank Pierce, over at Fort Laramie," Hill answered.

"I'm sorry... I don't think I know the individual you're referring to," Mason countered boldly.

"Hmmm... he said he knew you," Hill lied, checking the reaction of Broome to his statement.

Mason answered him calmly, "Well there are many people a public representative meets in the course of his duties, both civilian and military. Quite often the person assumes that a casual encounter somewhere brings more familiarity in the event than has actually occurred. What occasioned him to mention me?"

"Well he was in town the day she was attacked in the hotel. Sittin' here talkin' t' me as a matter o' fact," Hill responded.

"Yes and why should my name have entered the conversation?"

Sheriff Hill was good at recognizing a liar and he knew Broome was lying through his teeth. However, he was not a good liar himself and decided to face Broome with the issue.

"Now here's how I see it... Becky says ya knew she ran off with this feller... an' I think you've tried t' have 'er kilt fer it. I can connect the breed an' the three fools that got kilt here t' Fort Laramie…"

"Now just what do you mean?" Broome interjected, but before he could continue, Hill came back at him. "Jist shut up a fer a lousy minute! Personally I don't give a spit if ya did! She ain't dead. She ain't in my town anymore. An' she ain't my problem. But you ain't got them bounty hunters fooled neither!"

Broome remained silent now. His heart was racing. He steeled himself trying to remain calm and said, "If you believe all of this to be true, why are you telling me?"

Sheriff Hill smiled and walked to the door and locked it. Mason shifted uneasily in his seat. He was not accustomed to elected officials being crude with him and he feared that Hill was about to become violent when he locked the door.

Hill smiled again and said, "Now don't git yer nerves hot. I'm a believer in you scratch my back an' I'll scratch yers."

Mason calmed considerably as he recognized the unfolding of a familiar game. So, politics could be played on the frontier too he mused.

"Now, I probably could go t' all the trouble t'

prove conspiracy t' attempt murder if I had to... but, I'm a practical man. I got information them bounty hunters ain't got. A sheriff don't make a whole big lot... know what I mean?" Hill waited, watching intently for Broome's reactions.

Mason thought he knew exactly what Hill meant, but, he needed to make sure. "No, why don't you tell me exactly what you mean?"

"Okay, I'm gonna spell it out fer ya. I'm a town sheriff. Once I ain't got no problem in my town I ain't got no use fer the information I got... but them bounty hunters you hired do."

Mason carefully scrutinized Hill's expression. He had to be very careful. Almost anything he said would be an admission of guilt. He decided to probe further, "Yes, I can see how your jurisdiction enters in, but what do you mean? What are you proposing?"

"Don't try that slick eastern stuff with me," Hill leered. "You know I gotcha by the hairs. You must figger we're jist dumber th'n rocks out here. Well them men with her ain't dumb an' neither am I. It's a simple case o' how much work I wanna do. I'll take a thousand dollars t' keep what I know t' myself... ya don't pay an' I give the information t' them hard cases. Pure an' simple."

"Well," Mason began, "let's suppose you were correct in your assumption. How would one know that you hadn't already told them what you think?"

"They ain't no thinkin' to it. What I know is facts. I kin tie all four o' them dead fools ya hired t' Pierce. You give me some time with Pierce he'll spill his guts... an' you can trust yer momma t' that.

The difference b'tween me an' them bounty hunters is, they suspect the same thing... but they don't know how t' prove it... I do."

"But, if a person were to do as you suggest he would be admitting guilt," Mason replied.

"Don't mean a thing whether ya admit it 'r not... I kin prove it an' ya know it. If them other boys had anything, they'da nailed ya the second ya stepped off the train... the only thing that ties you t' this mess is Pierce, an' I'm the only one that knows who he is."

"Supposing you were right, what guarantee would I have that once I have paid the money you won't provide evidence against me anyway?" Mason queried.

"A man in yer situation ain't entitled t' guarantees," Hill responded, "but let me remind ya o' sumthin'... them fellas ain't been real concerned about takin' prisoners... 'r have ya thought about that?" Hill punctuated his last remark by poking Mason in the chest with his finger.

Mason Broome stood abruptly and asked, "Tell me sheriff, what does Becky believe?"

"She ain't no fool neither," he answered.

Mason lowered his eyes, making his best attempt at contrition. "I've made a horrible mistake," Mason began his lie, "I only came to realize just how horrible on the trip out here. Now... I'm not convinced that you could make your case sheriff, nor am I convinced that if you gave what you believe to be incriminating evidence that it would hold up. I am concerned about Becky. To spare her I am willing to buy your silence."

He looked up to see what effect he was having so far. Sheriff Hill looked annoyed. "I have funds on deposit here in Cheyenne, to cover expenses. As soon as the bank opens in the morning I'll make arrangements for you to be paid. All I want is a chance to start again with my wife." Mason moved immediately to the door, unbolted it, and stepped into the darkness.

The sheriff sat on the edge of his desk and rolled a cigarette. He lit up, blew a cloud of smoke, and said aloud, "Yeah, you fancy pants... I bet yer concerned about yer wife." He walked to the door and watched as Mason Broome crossed the dark street toward the hotel.

Tuck met Mason in the lobby as Mason entered the hotel.

"We're all set fer in the mornin'," Tuck informed him.

"Fine, I must stop briefly at the bank before we leave. I know that will make us get off to a slightly later start but it can't be helped," Mason replied.

"What'd ol' Hill have t' say that took so long?" Tuck inquired.

"Not much more than you had told me. It just took him longer to say it," Mason said with a convincing grin, and he bid Tuck a good night.

As Mason climbed the stairs he was seething inside. Becky had not only cost him his honor and reputation, she had cost him monetarily, and the cost had soared again tonight. Even as angry as he was, an inner voice screamed to him, pay the money, get back on the train, and leave her to her own devices. But, Mason Broome was not a man who could forgive and forget. He could not just return to Kentucky.

CHAPTER 16

The first two days on the trail back to the ranch were rather uneventful for Jim and Becky. Jim's occasional attempts to make small talk were marginally successful. They spent both nights camped under the stars with Becky sleeping on one side of the fire and Jim on the other. Becky would roll up in her blankets after supper and sleep silently until morning.

Jim had lain awake both nights staring up at the stars. He needed to remain extra vigilant since he couldn't count on the extra eyes and ears of his partner.

As the dew settled it had a way of enhancing the aroma of the plant life surrounding them. He took deep breaths of the cold night air. He was glad to be out in the open country again. But, he had to be careful never to admit that to Tuck.

On the third morning Jim announced, "We'll be in Crayt t'night. I s'pose ole Bert's still got room in the barn. Tell ya what though, this time o' year sleepin' in a barn kin be colder than sleepin' near a fire out in the open."

"Can't we just go on to the ranch?" she asked.

"It's another half day's ride t' the ranch, besides we need t' pick up enough provisions t' last awhile. Ain't no tellin' what, if anything, or who, is left at the ranch."

"Why do you say that?" she asked. "We've only been gone a short time."

"Yeah, well when a place is deserted an' anybody knows about it, ya kin always figger that somebody's gonna go an' help hisself t' what's left... I doubt if Vogel would sit still for that. He's probably figured that when we pulled out with you, we had what we came for and he is in the clear. Problem is, we just won't know til we git there. I doubt if anyone ever expected you t' be comin' back."

"Including you I presume," she said icily.

Jim laughed and said, "Me in p'ticular."

"I take it you think I'm quite daft for coming back here," Becky ventured.

Jim looked at her for a moment and then replied, "If daft means what I think it does, I figgered ya fer that long afore we started this trip," and, in his typically disarming fashion, laughed uproariously. He knew he shouldn't have said it, but he just couldn't resist. What the heck, in a few days, he and Tuck could ride off and forget the whole thing.

Becky's mouth was open in astonishment. Suddenly she burst forth with laughter herself, taking Jim totally by surprise.

"Well my, my! She does have a laugher in there!" Jim noted with obvious glee and approval.

Becky slapped him sharply but playfully on the arm and retorted, "Well I haven't exactly had much to laugh about now have I?"

Jim pulled the team up abruptly shouting, "Whoa!" He jumped down from the seat and ran a few steps as though he were afraid of her exclaiming, "Lord have mercy, two humor fits in a row!"

Becky eyed him maliciously for a moment, but she was laughing as she commanded, "Get back up here you fool!"

As Jim climbed back in the seat he said, "Becky, you are indeed a woman of mystery."

"And, don't you ever forget it," she replied saucily.

"Oh my!" Jim blurted and whipped the team into a trot. "Becky, where've ya been?"

"What do you mean?" she asked in return.

"I mean, once in awhile ya kin be like what I think yer normal self prob'ly is, an' then ya go away inside yerself. When're ya comin' out fer good?"

Becky looked off across the broad expanse of open land. The sun was brilliant and the dry grass reflected the gold of its light. The sky was deep blue. Wispy white clouds floated high above her. In her mind she asked, *Yes Becky, when are you coming out for good?* It was a beautiful day, and yet she was so inwardly troubled that it was difficult to enjoy the moment.

"I've been abused by a man I fell in love with

and by many other men at his hands. I've had two attempts made to kill me. I had to kill one of the men who was trying to kill me... planned by my husband, or Klaus, I'm not sure. Tuck is bringing Mason out here to force me to face him and we will in all likelihood have a showdown with Klaus... and you wonder why I'm withdrawn."

She was already beginning to withdraw again and Jim hastened to prevent it. He reached over and placed his arm around her and pulled her to him. She slid next to him without hesitation and laid her head on his shoulder.

"Becky, I ain't a serious braggin' man. Oh, I brag all the time but I do it fer fun. I wanna tell ya sumthin' though. Me an' Tuck'll kill the fool that tries to abuse ya no matter who it is. An' like you said, you killed one yerself. I know you've had it bad. Yer husband is yer husband, but he's gonna have t' take us straight on t' hurt ya now an' trust me, we ain't gonna allow it. And if Vogel is there, he's in for another big surprise."

Becky snuggled closer to him. She wore no perfume on the trail but Jim's senses were tantalized by her essence. He pulled her to him more tightly and she responded warmly.

That evening when they arrived in Crayt, Jim pulled the carriage into the corral area next to the barn. He and Becky stepped down and walked up the hill to the store where Bert still had a light burning.

Bert refused to listen to any talk of Becky sleeping in the barn again and he made his own accommodations available to her.

Later that night, after Becky had gone to bed, Jim informed Bert of the attempts made upon Becky's life since leaving Crayt. Bert insisted that Jim remain in the warmth of the store area with him and Becky. Bert and Jim slept on pallets on the floor.

The next morning Jim was up early loading supplies in the carriage and hitching the team in preparation for the trip to the ranch. He heard movement in the barn behind him and turned to see Becky standing just a few feet behind him. The sun was coming up and its radiance bathed her face in rose adding a rich luster to her complexion. She was fresh and combed. Her eyes sparkled as Jim beheld her in the morning glow.

"Bout ready t' go," Jim said dryly, trying to mask the true nature of his feelings for her at that moment. Jim had tried to think of all the reasons why he should not be having thoughts of Becky like this. None of those reasons were prevailing.

Becky had a blanket around her shoulders to shield her from the morning cold. Her hair lay upon her shoulders in strawberry swirls that reflected the red of the morning sun. She smiled at Jim and said teasingly, "May I sit close to you again today?"

Jim's pulse quickened. Trying not to read too much into what might after all just be a joke, he replied, "I think the owner of the rig gits t' sit wherever she wants."

Becky tossed her hair and laughed. "And, the owner wants to sit as close to the driver as she can."

Jim led the team and rig out of the barn and helped Becky into the seat. As he climbed up and seated himself Becky slipped her arm around him and snuggled close to him.

It was another gorgeous morning. Birds sang melodically as a giant red-orange ball climbed gradually higher in the sky promising to shed its warmth over the open expanse of grassland. In the cold morning brilliance the team plodded through clouds of shimmering vapor created by their breath as they pulled the carriage from the barn to the road leading southward to the ranch. The sun glinted brightly off their hooves made wet by the early morning dew.

Meadowlarks, startled by their approach, soared low over the grass. Their yellow breasts were brilliant in the morning sun.

Normally on the trail Jim's thoughts were largely of the joys awaiting him when he finally got to a town. Had he missed the experience of this kind of day all of his life, or was it the experience of Becky nestled closely to him that had heightened his exhilaration with this particular day?

"Jim, you've known I've had strong feelings for you all along haven't you?" Becky asked, breaking the silence.

Jim resisted the temptation to reply that he did know her feelings for him were strong but hadn't known whether they were favorable or not. Instead, he replied cautiously, "Why me an' not Tuck? If it weren't fer him comin' out here t' git ya, I wouldn't be here."

"I don't know... Tuck remembers a schoolgirl and that's who he came after. She doesn't exist anymore. And, even if I did have feelings for Tuck, he's cut from the same bolt of cloth that Mason is. He could never deal with what has happened to me."

"What makes ya think I could?" Jim asked with genuine interest.

Becky laughed aloud and replied, "Because Jim Link, you are what you are, and you don't expect anyone else to be anything but what they are."

"Well I 'spect yer right about that... but, who are you Becky, in yer own opinion?"

"I'm a woman who married for the wrong reasons. I'm a woman who fell in love with a despicable beast, and, I'm a woman who has paid a whale of a price for being ignorant."

Jim jumped slightly in mock astonishment at her use of an invective and exclaimed, "Lordy, she's got a sense a humor, an' she's tough on herself!"

Becky laughed at him, and herself, replying, "I don't make a habit of it, but sometimes only certain words tell it well enough."

Jim was rapidly gaining a new regard for this woman. Until yesterday he had been convinced that Becky would never be quite right and certainly always unpredictable.

"You know I've been so torn inside, worrying about what everyone will think of me... worrying what Mason will say or try to do to me... until finally I decided I've had enough! That's why I wanted to come back here," Becky continued.

"Why exactly is that?" Jim queried.

"Because on that ranch is my only chance to take control of my life again. It's where I lost control and where I'm convinced I'll find it again."

Jim wasn't exactly sure what Becky was planning, but at least she was in a feisty mood and that was healthy.

"I'm not going back with Mason, I don't care what he says! I would never trust him. I wish I had just told Tuck to turn him around and send him home."

"It ain't that easy darlin'," Jim said in a caring, almost fatherly, tone, "if he's gone this far he ain't likely to be so easy to stop til he gits satisfaction 'r whatever he came for. If he's behind it, we have t' play this thing out."

They drove on in silence for the next hour each having lapsed into their own thoughts.

Becky was first to speak asking Jim, "Have you ever thought of settling down to a family way of life?"

Well there it is he thought to himself. He had known all along that this wasn't the same as chasing whores in the saloons. A woman like Becky expected a commitment and a man like him preferred to play games. "You don't mind if I think about that a little b'fore I say anythin' do ya?" he said, smiling at her.

"Jim, I'm sorry that wasn't fair to you."

"No, that's alright, I jist wanna make sure that what I say is what I really mean t' say."

After a few minutes Jim made his response. "I've tried settlin' down twice. Didn't work very long fer me. Course the only reason I did the first time is cuz I thought I was s'pose to. The second time, me and Tuck tried cattle ranchin.' We didn't like it and the only reason we had fer stayin' in it was t' make money. I ain't never been a slave t' money... Guess what I'm sayin' is, so far I ain't had a real good reason. If I did, it might be different."

Jim wanted to be truthful. He never figured himself to be the settled down kind, but he wanted to keep the door open.

"Do you think I could be a good enough reason?" she asked coyly.

"Becky, do we hear what we're sayin? I mean, I know we're feelin' things, but, doncha think we better take 'er a little bit easy?

"You're right Jim. We'll just have to wait and see," she said flirtatiously as she pulled herself closer to him.

When they arrived at the ranch, Jim noticed there were still horses in the corral and that the water tank was nearly full. Somebody was tending to things. He studied the house for a long time looking for any signs of life. He knew Tuck would want him to wait, but it wasn't going to be easy to do that out in the open with Becky along. Vogel really should have been his for the taking the last time he and Tuck were here. If Vogel were here now, Jim would just take care of unfinished business. He instructed Becky to stay on the carriage seat as he pulled up to the house. He stepped down and walked toward the massive doors on the front of the house. Finding the doors unlocked, he entered, and found no one. He helped Becky down from the carriage and into the house.

Jim unpacked the supplies from the carriage setting them on the ground and drove the team down to the huge barn to search it. There was no one in the barn but there were signs that someone had been tending the horses.

Jim went to inspect the bunkhouse assuming one of the hands had stayed behind. There was no one in the bunkhouse and it showed no signs of recent occupancy. He concluded that it had to be Vogel tending to things.

Jim unhitched the team, unpacked the packhorses, and stowed the carriage in its place. He spent time with the team, the sorrel, and the gray, talking to them, rubbing them down, and currying their coats. He stood back and eyed the sorrel mare critically.

"Whiskey... that's a good name... ya got good color, yer a sight fer sore eyes, an yer a good companion on the trail. An' yer female... women and whiskey... ya gotta be careful at all times how ya handle 'em."

When he returned to the house to join Becky, he found her upstairs. She had made a fire in the cook stove downstairs and had heated some water in a pot. She was busily scrubbing the room that had been hers. When she saw Jim standing at the door she stopped and looked at him for a moment.

"You are probably wondering why I am doing this."

"No, I reckon I know."

"Good, then if you don't mind, in that bedroom down the hall you will find a bed with some chairs assembled around it."

Jim knew which room she meant.

"I would appreciate it if you would take everything in that room outside and burn it for me."

Her lower lip quivered as she fought back the tears. Her hair was wet from perspiration and curled close to her face. She stood there, small and brave, with a scrub brush in one hand, a bar of lye soap in the other, and a pot of water at her feet. Jim left without a word.

He rolled up the mattress and pushed it out the window and it fell to the ground outside. He carried each of the chairs down the steps and placed them in front of the fireplace in the great room. He left the bed's framework where it stood.

He took some kindling wood outside and set the mattress aflame thinking to himself that if someone were around, the fire would certainly arrest their attention. Maybe it would draw Vogel out.

He went back inside, broke the chairs down, and piled the wood in the fireplace. The inside of the house was cold and there was no sense letting the wood go to waste.

Jim set about organizing his belongings. He made a pallet of blankets on the floor of the great room. He'd be good and warm tonight next to the fireplace.

He rummaged around in the kitchen and found some coffee and a coffee pot. After stoking the fire in the cook stove he soon had the house filled with the aroma of brewing coffee. He sliced bacon off the slab in their supplies and soon had it frying in a pan on the stove. He had checked the kitchen carefully and it appeared that someone was indeed, at least on a frequent basis, living in the house.

Jim went upstairs to check on Becky. She was

still scrubbing. He inquired if she'd like to come down and eat. She declined saying what she had to do must be taken care of first and it would probably be several hours before she was finished. He went back downstairs.

Jim knew there were some things about a woman a man would simply never fully understand. But, he knew enough to leave her alone. In his own way, he understood that Becky's cleansing actions upstairs were an outward part of the inward work. She needed to be rid of every vile thing in her past to the furthest extent possible.

Rummaging around some more, Jim came upon a great beaten brass tub in a room just off the kitchen. Vogel's shaving brush and mug, his razor, and a bar of bath soap were stored neatly on a shelf. It looked like it had seen recent use.

Jim found as many buckets as he could and carried them full of water into the house. He placed every cooking utensil that would hold water on the top of the cook stove and began heating water for his bath.

Becky came down to find the top of the stove covered with containers of water. Without a word to Jim she refilled her pot and trudged back upstairs.

Jim took the buckets to the well and refilled them. Next he poured all of the containers of hot water into the tub and refilled each of them placing them back on the stove making sure that Becky was supplied with plenty of hot water. Jim closed the door of the side room and eased himself into the warm water to soak.

It was late at night when Jim threw the last of

the furniture wood on the fire and a couple of pieces of split log from the woodpile to bank the fire until morning. Finally, he could crawl into his blankets by the fireplace. The last things he heard as he drifted off to sleep were the crackling of the fire and muffled sounds upstairs as Becky continued her task.

In the morning Jim was up before dawn. He splashed water on his face from one of the pots on the stove. The fire in the cook stove was all but gone out and much of the water had evaporated but it was still warm. Jim added kindling to the coals until they blazed into a fire. Then he tossed in a few larger pieces from the supply by the side of the stove.

Jim thought of the many mornings on the trail when he'd shaken himself from his blankets and had gotten up stiff and sore from sleeping on the ground. He smiled inwardly thinking, *Jimbo, you're getting old*.

He thought of how many times the closeness of his room at a boardinghouse had driven him into the night just to get out. Winter or summer it was the same. It was only a place to sleep.

Jim had never known a real home. He never knew his father. His mother had been reduced to cleaning a bordello in order to feed the two of them. She died of consumption when Jim was four years old and he'd been raised as a community project among the prostitutes and the madam.

Jim was about ten years old when he learned through the conversation of the prostitutes that his own mother had been a member of that society until she became ill. Jim's mother had been a favorite of the madam and it was she who provided the means to raise Jim.

By the time Jim was thirteen he was on a first name basis with many of the male hierarchy in New Orleans who were regular customers of the house. He learned to use guns and knives, and picked up gambling skills from every man willing to teach him.

When he was fifteen, he confronted a man who was abusing one of the prostitutes. The man cursed him and Jim challenged the man openly by telling him that it might be easy to abuse a woman, but he asked him did he have the guts to face him?

The man was a lawyer and was entertaining friends and business acquaintances with an evening of house pleasures. The lawyer carried a derringer in his vest pocket and a long thin knife in a scabbard sewn into the side of his boot. Jim was armed with an old army revolver stuck in his waistband. One of the girls had come by it when two soldiers had fought over her. The soldier she was with had been killed by the other. When his body was removed from her room the soldier's belt, holster, and revolver still hung on the bedpost. Jim asked her for them and she had given them to him. The room had fallen silent that night. There was murder in the lawyer's eyes and his face was scarlet with embarrassment as he rose to face Jim.

Although Jim had never faced a man in a gunfight before, his teacher's had taught him well. Watch the man's eyes and never let your own betray your move.

Jim had seen the lawyer's face jerk spasmodically. Jim drew his pistol as the lawyer's hand darted inside his coat.

Jim drew and fired in one fluid motion just as he had been taught. The bullet struck the lawyer squarely in the face and the derringer's muffled report followed. The lawyer's hand was still inside his coat.

Jim fled to the north and joined the U.S. Army. There was no one to vouch for his age and no way to challenge it. He was tall for his age and the recruiting sergeant was impressed with his grit. When the civil war began two years later Jim stayed with the union. He met Tuck when they were both prisoners of war.

Jim had been staring out the window toward the barn, mulling over his past, when he saw a rider approaching. He poured himself a cup of reheated coffee from the previous night's pot.

When the rider was close enough to identify Jim went outside to meet him. Vogel reined his horse up short. Sensing something wrong, he wheeled the horse and rode away before he was within range.

CHAPTER 17

Tuck and Mason got a late start the first day because of Mason's business at the bank. To make up a little time they galloped their horses awhile then let them walk. After the horses were rested they put them at a trot for a time then slowed to a walk again. Under these conditions conversation was only sporadic.

They continued to ride throughout the day eating in the saddle from the light provisions Tuck had packed that morning in the saddlebags.

Mason could understand why Tuck was pressing to get down the trail, but speaking for himself, he still needed time to plan his actions.

Tuck occasionally probed Mason, trying to bring him into a conversation that would lead to a frank discussion of his actions toward Becky. So far it had been Mason doing most of the talking, endeavoring to provide Tuck with plausible reasons why he had felt it necessary to intentionally mislead him concerning Becky's true predicament. It all sounded lame to Tuck and he was convinced that Mason was lying.

They finally stopped in late afternoon to make camp. The days were getting shorter and Tuck hated fooling around in the dark trying to get a camp set up. Besides, he was tired from pressing all day to make time, and if he was tired, Mason certainly was.

Mason had no real trail experience although he was a good horseman. It fell Tuck's lot to make camp and cook. He missed Jim. He and Jim knew what to do without having to talk about it.

Tuck soon had things in shape and he and Mason sat by the fire watching the beans heat. Tuck carved thick slices from a slightly deformed loaf of bread he had tried to pack carefully among the provisions on the packhorse. Tuck had made arrangements with Sheriff Hill to use the dead man Cline's mount as a packhorse until they returned to Cheyenne.

The hot beans and fresh bread were satisfying after a long day in the saddle. The coffee finished brewing about the time they downed the last morsels of food.

Mason was leaned back against his saddle. "You know Tuck, sometimes I wish I could walk away from all my responsibilities and live a simpler life."

Tuck poured coffee for both of them and handed a cup to Mason. "That's cuz it ain't rainin', sleetin', 'r snowin' right now. Life ain't near as simple then."

Mason laughed and said, "Yes, those could be drawbacks out here. But still... there's a peace and tranquility out here that in my world is unobtainable."

"Yeah I think I know what ya mean," Tuck said. "I'm 'bout sick t' my guts o' bein' involved in everyone else's problems. I'd live out here somewhere by m'self, but the Indians is the best there is at survivin' out here, an' I hear they're starvin' unless they take the government handouts. Game is scarce and hiders have pretty much killed off the Buffalo."

Mason covered up with his blankets and stretched out on the thick prairie thatch. Resting on the saddle, he gazed up at the darkening sky. The night was clear and cold. Soon the sky would be ink black and filled with innumerable glimmering golden specks. He took a sip of the freshly brewed coffee. "Men have made themselves slaves to their own desires. It takes money to get what you want and then it takes money to keep it. And, there's always someone waiting in the wings to jump in and take over if you can't keep up."

Tuck turned Mason's last comment over in his mind for a few moments and then commented, "Man has t' count what he's willin' t' do jus' t' keep up. If someone's waitin' t' take over my job he'll find me mighty glad t' let him have it."

Mason was soon snoring. Tuck walked over and removed the cup from Mason's hand and threw out its contents. He shook his head in mild contempt. You would never have walked up to Jim Link like that and him not even know you were there.

The next day they were on the trail early. As they rode along Tuck decided it might be a good time for a head on approach concerning Becky. "Mason, I wanna tell ya somethin' straight out. I got strong suspicions 'bout you arrangin' attempts t' kill yer wife... I'd like t' hear whatcha got t' say about that."

Mason did his best to look astonished even though he was acutely aware that Tuck had been pressing to this point since they had begun their journey. "Gracious Tuck! How could you think such a thing? Now why would I go to all the trouble to have her rescued from Klaus if that were true?"

"Well, it'd sure make a good cover if anything happened t' her durin' the process wouldn't it?" was Tuck's response. "Who else would be a tryin' it? Fer what reason?"

"Tuck, I hate to talk about my own wife this way but let me ask you something. Is she not a beautiful woman? A woman who, if all reports I've heard are true, is now quite experienced in ways that the men out here would find highly desirable. You are only assuming they were trying to kill her. I think they were trying to take her back to Klaus Vogel!" Mason's face was a mask as he gazed at Tuck, but inside, he was quite pleased with the passion he'd mustered for his last remarks.

"Yeah, we thought about that some too," Tuck said calmly. Mason's remark about Becky's experiences had reminded Tuck of the details she had revealed to him that night on the way to Cheyenne. Something inside of him recoiled at the remembrance.

"Why in the world would I be riding all this way to meet her on her own terms? Does she think I owe her that? Listen Tuck, I'm not at all sure what I'll find when I see Becky, but believe me, if I'd wanted her dead I'd have had it done long ago," Mason continued.

"Mebbe," Tuck said, unconvinced, "but let me tell ya this, if it was you... I'd kill ya jis' like I'd flick a fly. We clear on that?"

Mason's heart was pounding. The deadly calm with which Tuck had delivered the warning was unnerving. Mason forged ahead anyway with all the false bravado he could muster. "I have no fear of you Spence. And, I'll kindly remind you that you are on my payroll. My only intent is to take my wife home where she belongs!"

Tuck reined his horse to a stop and Mason reined in as well. Tuck turned in the saddle and faced Mason squarely. "Let me remind ya Mason... you ain't back east now... out here in the open country, the law is what I say it is... an' there's been a lots o' men that wasn't afraid o' me... I'm still standin' an' they ain't." Tuck spurred the roan and rode off down the trail ahead of Mason.

He was troubled within himself. He'd played the encounter badly. It was obvious he wasn't equipped to try out talking Mason Broome. He'd hoped to corner him in a lie, but Mason lied with such confidence and ease that cornering him wasn't going to be a simple matter. Tuck had never needed to rely much on talk to make things happen. At least things were out in the open now. If push came to shove, he had warned him.

Mason stayed well behind Tuck for the remainder of the day. After his confrontation with Sheriff Hill, and now with Tucker Spence, he had learned these frontier men were markedly different from those he knew in his own society.

In Mason's world arbitration, compromise, and argument were the everyday tools of engagement between foes. Spence and Hill were both blunt and ill-tempered men, and definitely not ignorant. He realized he had greatly underestimated Tucker Spence and was totally unprepared for his directness.

Tuck never once looked around to see if Mason was following on the buckskin. He knew he was there just the same.

That night when they camped they both turned in early. Nothing was said between them except what was absolutely necessary.

Tuck slept very lightly that night with his Colt lying across his stomach under his blankets. Now that he had confronted Mason there was no need for either of them to be coy.

The next morning they were close enough to Crayt to arrive by early afternoon. Tuck said to Mason, "You ride ahead t'day. I'll bring up the rear."

Mason looked at him questioningly, but since he had no desire to engage Tuck in conversation after the accusations of the previous day, he mounted the buckskin and rode off.

"Jus' stay on the trail, it goes right in t' town," Tuck called before Mason was out of earshot.

It was about three o'clock in the afternoon when Tuck rode up alongside Mason and pointed to the hitching rail in front of the saloon.

"We'll stop in there an' cut the dust," Tuck said.

They stopped in front of the saloon and dismounted. When they entered the saloon Jack greeted Tuck with a loud and cordial, "Hey! Kinda figgered you'd stop in here. Bert told us yer pardner was through and said you'd be comin' along."

"They got here okay then?" Tuck responded.

"Looked okay t' Bert."

"This here's Mason Broome. He's travelin' out t' the ranch with me. We could use a drink."

"Comin' right up," Jack said as he rose from the table and took his place behind the bar. He poured Tuck a beer and Mason a shot of whiskey.

"Come sit down," Pete called to the pair.

Tuck picked up his mug and Mason his glass and the two stepped over to join the ranchers.

"Yer from back east ain't ya?" Pete inquired of Mason.

"Yes, I am. I own property in Kentucky and I am a representative of that state in the federal government," Mason stated proudly.

"That little woman the German had... I heard she had a husband back east. You him?" Pete asked craftily.

Tuck reached over and placed his hand lightly on Pete's arm and said, "Pete, a genuine Texas fortune teller don't need t' be askin' questions. What's more, certain things ain't yer business." Tuck was smiling as he said it but Pete got his drift immediately.

Mason's face was crimson making it quite obvious that Pete had hit the nail on the head. Pete's remark resurrected the indignation within Mason. If there had been times when he entertained the thought that perhaps he could make amends with Becky and that things could be made right again, this crude old rancher had settled that issue for him. He neither knew, nor did he care to know, the people in this town. But, if the public's knowledge concerning Becky had embarrassed him so out here, he knew he could never live it down in Kentucky or Washington.

Tuck saw that Mason was extremely uncomfortable. *Good*, he thought, *serves him right.* Yet, there was turmoil within him too. Pete's remark had made Tuck wonder just how much of what went on at that ranch was public knowledge now. He was embarrassed himself to think of it.

"Well then let's jist git on t' sumthin' important. One o' the hands from Vogel's ranch came through here, said you boys were really sumthin' takin' Race and Soto down," Ned interposed.

"What kinda sumthin?" Tuck asked.

"C'mon, you know what I'm talkin' about. Tell us how it started when ya went out there," Ned pried.

Tuck came back with a question: "What'd the cowhand say happened?"

"He jist told us the end o' things. What started it?" Ned replied.

Tuck took a long pull on his beer and said deferentially, "I 'spect ya better ask Jim about that... he had more t' do with it than I did."

"Might as well tell 'em Tuck. They'll hound ya til ya do," Jack said from behind the bar.

Tuck wasn't big on story telling. He decided to make an exception in this case for two reasons: First, because Mason was there. Tuck figured it might do him good to hear firsthand what he was up against now that he could be held personally accountable for any acts against Becky. Second, because Jim was the principal player in the story and it wouldn't sound like Tuck was trying to brag.

When he had finished it was obvious the story and the swiftness of its events had a telling effect upon all the listeners.

It was Pete who finally spoke. "They hung that boy," he said in disbelief.

"Yeah, we were too late t' stop it," Tuck answered.

Mason was taken aback to think that no one even got a shot off except for Tuck and Jim and that it was over in an instant. He had previously pictured some kind of running gun battle with Tuck and Jim taking the ranch in a manner similar to those he'd heard about during the civil war.

It disappointed Mason to think that Klaus didn't even know who Tuck and Jim were or why they had come.

Tuck broke in upon Mason's thoughts with a proposal.

"Ya know it's about six 'r seven hours t' the ranch with a wagon 'r a buggy. We can cut miles off, now that I know exactly where it is, by ridin' cross country. If we left now we'd be there by about ten o'clock. I'd rather push on than spend the night here."

Mason agreed and the two men left the saloon.

They mounted their horses and rode off just as the sun was setting. The buckskin fell in alongside the roan and Tuck made no objection.

When darkness fell the sky was clear and a bright full moon lighted the trail ahead. The two men rode alongside without talking. It was cold enough that both men had donned the coats they carried tied beneath their bedrolls.

The natural sounds of the night played melodies in Tuck's ears as he listened intently for any sound out of the ordinary. They turned off the trail and began their cross-country trek. The blowing of the horses and the creaking of saddle leather added to the symphony of the night as they made their way up and down the slopes.

It's probably not possible, Tuck thought to himself, *but the best thing that could happen would be if Becky and Mason could work out their differences and go home together in peace.* Then he and Jim could ride off in the opposite direction in peace.

Although he was still protective of Becky, Tuck had reconciled within himself that whatever her future was he wasn't going to be part of it. The more he thought about it the better he felt about it. He and Jim had always wanted to go to the Oregon territories. Spring would be a good time to just take off and go. He was anxious to get this thing over with, so he and Jim could get on with their own plans

It was late afternoon, on the second day of their stay at the ranch, when Becky finally announced to Jim that her cleaning tasks were complete. She'd spoken very little to him and he'd refrained from intruding upon her. "Is there enough water left for me?" she inquired. She looked exhausted.

"Yep, I've filled 'em every time ya emptied 'em," Jim replied, pointing toward the pots on the cook stove.

Before entering the room off the kitchen she paused at the door and spoke to Jim. "Would you mind... not being in the house while I'm in here?" she asked. Her tone was apologetic.

Jim peered across the room at the bedraggled little figure, wet with perspiration and scrub water. "I wouldn't mind Becky. I understand."

"And, do you see Jim? I was sure you would, without me having to explain. Mason wouldn't... neither would Tuck." She entered the side room and closed the door.

Jim went outside as agreed closing the door loudly enough to give her confidence that she was alone and would not be disturbed. He thought it best not to tell her that he'd seen Vogel approaching the ranch.

For a long time he stood leaning on the corral rail contemplating what it would be like to live permanently in one place with one woman.

Whiskey nuzzled under the rail at Jim's pocket expecting a reward. Dusty stretched his neck over the mare's back, seeking attention as well.

"Yeah, I s'pose you two'd enjoy the chance t' git fat an' lazy."

A half hour before sunset, Becky called to him from the front door of the house. She was wearing a fresh blue and white checked dress. Her skin was pink from the scrubbing she'd given herself and her hair, still partially damp, hung in ringlets. She looked and smelled delicious. "Do you like potatoes and onions fried together in a skillet?" she asked, eyes wide with anticipation.

He'd never seen her eyes dance as they did now.

"I found everything we need and there's a ham in the smokehouse." Her voice bubbled with excitement.

Jim laughed and replied, "Stuff fit fer a king."

She took his arm and led him into the house. Looking around mischievously, as a child would do prior to the execution of a well-planned prank, she said, "I was never allowed to do anything in the kitchen... except what I was told." Her voice was a whisper as though Klaus might be listening. "I wonder where he is."

"Well darlin', you kin darn sure do whatever ya want now," Jim reassured her, ignoring her question. Jim insisted on helping Becky and soon the two were laughing and joking at his efforts to peel potatoes with his Louisiana skinning knife.

"It would be nice if there were something left to slice and fry!" Becky chided.

"I'm jis' lookin' out fer ya by cuttin' off the part that makes you gals fat!" he returned.

The aroma of the meal cooking on the wood stove aroused their appetites. After supper Becky turned to Jim to ask, "Do you mind if I leave the dishes until morning?" It was a domestic question; a question that might be asked by any wife of any husband. The question had a strange effect upon Jim. He wasn't sure why. Things seemed to be heading in a particular direction faster than he was comfortable with. Her question suggested a settled intimacy that Jim simply wasn't ready for.

"I told ya Becky. You kin do whatever ya want."

Becky made no response but walked into the great room and retrieved a lantern. With a lighted stick of kindling from the fire in the cook stove, she touched the flame to the wick of the lamp. Replacing the ornamental glass flue, she carried the lantern into the living room. She slid two large ornate rocking chairs side by side, sat in one, and motioned for Jim to sit in the other.

When Jim joined her she reached out and took his hand. Becky leaned her head back in the chair, closed her eyes, and began to rock gently in the chair. The two were soon rocking in unison. Hours passed before either of them spoke. All of the time Jim knew that he should be outside on guard in the event that Vogel was returning. It was Jim who finally broke the silence.

"Been meanin' t' ask ya, sorta waitin' fer the right time... you okay about havin' t' kill Cline?"

"Okay in what way?" she asked. Her eyes were still closed and she continued to rock gently in the chair.

"Well, I mean, ya don't need t' feel bad about it, if ya do, cuz he wasn't worth spit an' he deserved it."

Several moments went by in silence and then Becky replied, "I don't know what you'll think of me, but I was glad the next day. I mean it was like taking revenge on every man... every animal I should say... that disgraced me."

Jim studied her face. A tear coursed its way down her cheek. He rose from the chair and walked to the cook stove. Pouring himself a cup of coffee, he asked her if she'd have one with him. She declined. Jim sat down again in the chair beside her and took her hand.

"Can you tell me something?" Without waiting for his reply she continued, "Somehow I know you understand what I've gone through and what I'm going through... and yet I know Tucker Spence hasn't the slightest notion. I know my husband will never understand. Why do you?.. What makes you different?"

"Well, I think mebbe yer husband knows and I

know that Tuck knows. He's jist gonna deal with it differently. I grew up different t' begin with. Learned a long time ago that jist cuz a flower gits stepped on it don't stop bein' a flower." Jim paused to sip coffee from the cup held in his other hand. "Most gals I've known ain't society folk, but they got hearts an' feelin's jist the same... An, some I knew'd been purty high b'fore life knocked 'em down. Some fellers figger if a woman brings trouble on herself then she deserves what she gits." Jim turned to Becky looking directly into her eyes and smiled. "I always figgered any little girl with a skinned knee needed some salve an' a kiss."

Becky squeezed his hand firmly and said, "You are a healing salve to me Jim... but, I'm still waiting for the kiss."

A wicked little grin spread itself across Jim's face and he said, "Yeah, but there must be a better time than when we both jist ate onions."

Becky squealed with astonished laughter. She slapped him hard across the shoulder and cried, "You wretch!"

She jostled his arm so that the coffee almost spilled. He stood up and pulled Becky to her feet. The impish grin was still on his face as he said, "Awhile ago I saw a tear on yer face, I sorta had t' replace that with a smile."

He pulled her to him and kissed her gently on the lips. It was brief and tender, not an act of passion. To Jim, the kiss was an assurance to Becky that everything would work out okay. Holding her at arm's length he asked, "How's yer knee?"

"All better now," Becky replied huskily. For

her, the kiss had been something more.

Jim thought he heard noises outside.

Tucker Spence stood frozen in his tracks. He and Mason had just arrived in the dark. Fearing that, if alarmed, Jim might shoot first and ask questions later, Tuck had left Mason at the gate and was walking to the door to announce their arrival. The scene through the window by the light of the lantern had rendered him immobile. *So that's how it is*, he thought. He'd known it all along. Right from the beginning Becky was attracted to Jim and Jim used every chance to shine up to her. *Let them have each other then,* he said angrily to himself. He had for the most part given up on Becky anyway, but now, what he considered as Jim's betrayal of their friendship, was devastating to him.

"Well then its time t' face 'em on it," he said aloud and started for the door. Just as he was about to knock on the door he was reminded that Mason, Becky's husband, was standing at the gate waiting to see Becky who was inside with her lover. "What a stinkin' mess!" he said aloud as he banged on the door.

From inside Jim called out, "Who is it?"

"It's me bird brain!" Tuck replied impatiently.

Jim threw the door open and said with a big grin, "Well git in here then an' quit tellin' the neighbors all about me."

When Tuck entered the house he could see Becky standing in the middle of the great room.

Jim whomped Tuck on the back good naturedly and said, "Good t' see ya. Where's the husband?"

Jim's good nature and Becky's beauty were

both powerful mollifications for Tuck. He'd been mad at Jim a few times before but couldn't stay mad at him. He'd been sure that Becky was out of his system a couple of times before, but then he'd see her again.

"I left him with the horses down t' the gate."

Tuck was uncomfortable in that house now, just as before. Uncomfortable with the situation between Jim and Becky and uncomfortable with the pictures in his mind of what he'd found the last time he was here.

"I jist came up here t' make sure we ain't shot fer thieves... we're both beat from the ride, we'll put up in the bunkhouse an' see ya in the mornin'." Before Jim could object, Tuck turned and left closing the door behind him.

Affronted, Becky asked, "Did he seem a little sullen to you? He didn't even acknowledge my presence."

"Somethin's eatin' him," Jim answered.

When Tuck told Mason the two of them would spend the night in the bunkhouse Mason objected immediately. Mason had also observed the kiss through the window. He was at a much greater distance than Tuck and at first he wasn't sure. When he saw Tuck stop in his tracks and heard him muttering aloud he became positive.

"And, I suppose your friend will spend the night in the house with my wife!" he protested.

Tuck's mood was ugly and his patience thin.

"Well accordin' to yer version o' what she's become, what difference does one more make?" Tuck glared at Mason, waiting for any hostile reaction. It was a cheap thing to say about Becky and a cheap thing to say to her husband. But, Tuck wasn't about to apologize. The way he figured it everyone involved but him had already gotten in their cheap licks.

"My man, you're despicable," Mason said in disgust.

"Now, who do you think yer talkin' too, you cheap tinhorn?" Tuck spat, as his temper flared out of control.

Mason Broome was a cautious and calculating man who preferred to handle problems long distance. He was not a gunman and stood no chance against Tuck in a gunfight. However, he was not a coward, and in a fist fight could hold his own. "I've put up with your insolent mouth quite enough. If you're man enough to remove your weapons I think it's time you learned a thing or two!" Mason said evenly.

In the moment of his challenge to Tucker, Mason saw a possibility. It was a chance to get Tucker Spence out of the way if he'd take the bait.

"An' you think yer gonna teach me? Oh, this I gotta see," Tuck replied angrily.

Tuck unbuckled his gun belt, and as he turned to throw it over his saddle he said, "Step away from the horses an' let's git at it."

At the moment Tuck turned his back, Mason slipped Tuck's Winchester from its scabbard. Tuck was taken totally by surprise and clawed to retrieve the holster now hanging on the other side of the saddle. Then the night exploded in a thousand stars of every color. Mason had clubbed him hard with the rifle.

Mason dragged the unconscious Tuck into the shadows of the bunkhouse and out of the moonlight. Tuck's hat lay on the ground beside the horses and Mason could see that the yellow hair on the back of Tuck's head was dark and matted with blood.

Mason quietly retrieved the horses at the gate and walked them down to the bunkhouse tying them to the rail. Then he hunkered in the shadows beside Tuck who was lying motionless on the ground.

A few moments later, the burning lamp that had shone so revealingly through the window of the great house was extinguished.

Thirty minutes passed before Mason moved. He checked Tuck. Tuck's breathing was very shallow and he showed no signs of reviving. Mason thought about tying him up but checked himself. He had to make his move and make his getaway. Even if Tuck revived he'd be in no shape to protest what was going on.

Mason was exhausted and fatigue numbed his brain. He didn't really have a plan. He wasn't really sure what his intentions were when he assaulted Tuck, but now he had to begin some kind of action because the events were already in motion. He didn't relish the thought of hitting the trail again that night but he couldn't stop to rest. He forced himself into action.

He approached the house as quietly as he could. The front door was not locked. He'd never met Jim. But, if he were anything like Tucker Spence, Mason was sure that neither was the type who would lock the other out of a house. Suddenly a hand was over his mouth and he was being pulled over backwards. He felt a sharp stabbing pain between his shoulder blades and then darkness swept over him.

Klaus Vogel wiped the short sword on his trouser leg and returned it to the scabbard. He retrieved the Winchester that Mason had been carrying and entered the house silently. Peering into the great room he saw Jim's form, wrapped in blankets by the fireplace. He raised the rifle and took careful aim at Jim's back.

The muzzle report jolted Jim out of his sleep. He rolled out of his blankets scooping his Colt and gun belt off the floor. He flung himself into the darkness away from the fire's light.

"Jim! Jim!" It was Becky, her voice shrill with fear and excitement.

"What in blazes? Becky are ya alright? Where are ya? What happened?" Jim shouted.

"He's on the floor by the door! I'm upstairs."

Jim had no light to see by other than the fire. He listened intently for the sound of movement in the dark. He heard something at the top of the stairs.

"Becky if that's you movin' stop! Is it Mason 'r Tuck?"

Becky didn't answer but stopped moving.

Jim made his way in front of the windows around the outer perimeter wall and away from the giant opening leading to the foyer. It had to be Mason. Tuck had acted strangely, but Jim knew he wouldn't shoot them in the dark. "Tuck, are ya there?" There was no reply.

When he finally approached the opening he could see a Winchester lying on the floor and a hand clutching it. He stepped forward quickly and placed one foot squarely on the person's forearm while aiming his Colt at the body on the floor. There was no movement.

"Awright Becky, it's over. Come on down."

Having made sure the intruder was dead, Jim found a lantern and lit it. He brought the lantern close to the figure lying on the floor and turned him over. When the light revealed the features of the intruder, he heard Becky gasp, "Klaus!"

Jim's mind raced with questions. Where was Tuck? If Tuck had heard the shot he should be here by now. Vogel had been shot through the head. The bullet entered the upper right portion of the skull and exited his jaw on the left side of his face after passing through the brain. The skull had a huge entry wound and the jaw was completely shot away.

"Since I didn't do this, I figger you did, right?"

Becky nodded her head in the affirmative. She shuddered at the grisly sight while rubbing her shoulder; the recoil of the rifle had nearly knocked her down.

"What in the world did ya shoot 'im with?"

Becky ascended the stairs wordlessly and returned carrying Jim's .50 caliber Remington rifle.

"How did ya git this?"

"When you started snoring I just picked it up and took it upstairs with me."

Jim was surprised and embarrassed to think that Becky had sneaked up on him in the dark and spirited away one of his weapons.

As though she could read his thoughts, she explained, "I was barefoot, that's why you didn't hear me."

"We need t' find out what happened t' Tuck," Jim said urgently.

"Mason hit him over the head and dragged him down to the bunkhouse," Becky revealed.

"How do ya know that?"

"I was watching out the upstairs window when it happened. I was trying to see Mason... I haven't seen him for so long... I was curious. It all happened so quickly."

"Why didn't you tell me?" Jim asked in surprise.

"Well, I couldn't really tell if it was Tuck who hit Mason or the other way around. Then I saw Mason dragging Tuck toward the bunkhouse and I knew... I knew Mason had come to kill me himself."

"Yes, but this is Vogel not Mason. Where is Mason?"

Jim was fully dressed now, carrying the lantern, and on his way out the door to find Tuck. "But, why didn't ya call me?"

"Because this started between Mason and me. It had to finish between him and me... but I almost got you killed," Becky said as her voice shook with sobs. "After I came back upstairs with your rifle, I looked out and saw him coming toward the house. I was terrified. I wanted to scream for you... but I... for some reason I didn't... then he was inside aiming a rifle at you... I had to shoot him."

"What if you'da missed?"

"I didn't."

Jim stepped out the door and immediately

discovered Broome's body. He was obviously dead as well. *Oh no*, he thought, *I wonder what's happened to Tuck.*

CHAPTER 19

The sun was warm on Tuck's face. He opened his eyes and the pain from the light made him close them immediately. He turned his head away from the light and tried again. Gradually his eyes adjusted and he could look around. He had no idea where he was. The room was washed white and he could see blue sky through the panes of a large window at the foot of the bed. He turned his head back toward the light. It was the sun shining brightly through a window on his left. To his right a door was open to a hallway.

He tried raising himself on his elbows but an intense wave of pain in his head curtailed his effort. He moaned and fell back on the pillow. His head throbbed as waves of pain were accompanied by purple, gold, and red flashes behind his tightly closed eyes. Finally, the throbbing reduced to a dull ache and he reopened his eyes.

He heard footsteps in the hall outside. Turning

his head slightly he looked and saw Jim coming through the door.

"Well, by thunder ya ain't dead, are ya?" Jim said, in a voice loud enough to renew the pain.

Tuck made no immediate response waiting for the pulsations to subside. When once again the violent throb reduced to a dull ache he asked, "Where we at?"

"Well, we're at Vogel's ranch an' yer in Becky's bed."

Jim's words were enough to begin a flood of memories. The last thing Tuck remembered was that Mason had the Winchester.

"I got shot I guess," he ventured.

"No, Mason whacked ya on the head with yer rifle."

Suddenly Tuck remembered why Mason had come and a moment of panic seized him. "Is Becky alright?"

Jim gave a humorless laugh and said, "Yea, she's fine. I don't think she's near as helpless as you might think."

"What happened? Where's Mason? What…"

"Hold on!" Jim intervened. "Yer gonna git all het up. Jist lay still an' I'll fill ya in." Jim pulled a chair up and began relating the events that had taken place after Tuck was rendered unconscious. When Jim finished the part concerning Vogel killing Mason and Becky shooting Vogel, Tuck erupted.

"How's she takin' it!?"

"Well," Jim laughed dryly, "it ain't funny I guess, but, in a way it is. Let me tell ya."

"Could ya git me a drink o' water first? I'm parched... m' throat wants t' close up on me."

"Sure thing. I'll be right back."

When Jim returned with the water Tuck struggled to sit up. Jim hastened to help him and together they managed to get Tuck propped up on the pillows to a sitting position. Tuck took small swallows of water until his throat was moistened.

"How long have I been like this?"

"T'day's the third day... an I tell ya it's about time yer up... I've changed yer bed all I'm in the mood fer."

Tuck laughed, a little embarrassed, and the laughter provoked the throbbing.

Jim resumed the narration of events to Tuck. He had found Tuck lying in the dark and at first thought he was dead. When he saw that Tuck was alive, but unconscious, he carried him back to the house. Becky had insisted that Tuck be placed in her bed. While Becky attended to Tuck's wounds, Jim had carried Vogel outside.

"This whole thing has been crazy from the beginning," Tuck observed.

"Well, I once knew a man crazy enough t' believe a woman'd still be in love with a farmboy... an' then he rode half way t' Purgatory t' rescue 'er," Jim offered.

"If ya thought I wuz crazy, why'd ya come with me?"

Jim grinned and said, "Didn't know how crazy ya wuz til we got here."

Jim looked sheepishly at Tuck for a moment and then began, "Tuck I need t' tell ya. There's somethin' kinda botherin' me, an' I gotta git it off my chest. I got kind o' confused fer awhile. I maybe did some wrong thinkin' about me and Becky, an' I feel kinda guilty about it."

"Yeah, I figgered," Tuck stated flatly.

Jim rose and walked to the window. From Becky's window he could look out over the hills surrounding the home site. "Well, it might not be like ya think," Jim said defensively.

Tuck made no response.

After several moments of awkward silence Jim turned to face Tuck and said, "Well, ya ain't gonna believe what happened."

"Yeah, how's that?" Tuck asked.

Jim continued that while he and Becky were attending to Tuck, waiting for him to regain consciousness, they both concluded that Mason had been bent upon her destruction and would certainly have attempted it. It was Becky who came up with the idea of a death certificate. She insisted that Jim bury both Klaus Vogel and her husband Mason immediately and that a death certificate be drawn up to be signed by Jim and Bert, if Bert would, as witnesses that they were both dead.

When Jim returned from the burying and from Crayt with a frontier version of a death certificate, Becky was very distant with him.

Becky had searched the house until she found her Bible among the things she had not taken with her previously. She spent the remainder of that afternoon sitting in one of the rocking chairs reading.

That evening, after Jim had attended to the

horses, Becky called him to her side and asked him to read a passage from the Bible. It was from the gospel of St. John:

"... Woman, where are those, thine accusers? hath no man condemned thee? She said, No man, Lord. And Jesus said unto her, Neither do I condemn thee: go and sin no more."

When he finished reading, Becky explained to him that she had been an adulteress with Klaus and that Mason had been her accuser. She was not an adulteress now, and with Mason dead, she no longer had an accuser. Then she announced that she was going to return to Kentucky and to her home. "An' she left in the buggy this mornin', " Jim finished.

"What? Jim, she can't git t' Cheyenne by herself!" Tuck complained.

"Ha! That's what I said. She took me to a closet over in ole Klaus' room... showed me a strong box in there with more money th'n you kin b'lieve. Well, I got ole Bert t' sign the paper. I also signed a paper sayin' I had t' kill Mason m'self. I figgered that'd keep down a lot o' questions. I hired Pete t' take Becky t' Cheyenne. They left this mornin' bag and baggage."

Tuck looked away from Jim and stared out the window for a long time and then finally asked, "When are ya s'posed t' join 'er?"

It took Jim a moment to answer. "She didn't mention me comin' an' I didn't mention goin,'" Jim stated flatly.

The two men looked each other straight in the eye. Tuck didn't ask for, and didn't want to know, the details.

"What's she plannin' t' do with this ranch then?" Tuck asked in bewilderment.

Jim shook his head again and replied, "I ask 'er that. She said it's not hers and never was hers, but the one in Kentucky is... said if me an' you wanted it we could probably have it."

"That woman is sure hard t' figger," Tuck exclaimed.

Jim threw his head back and cried with glee, "Find me one that ain't!"

In the days that followed Tuck regained his strength. He spent several hours each day sitting outside in the crisp fall air letting the golden rays of the warm autumn sun add their virtue to healing the wound in his head. He was soon able to stand and walk without his head pounding in protest.

One evening, as he and Jim sat at the table in the kitchen, Tuck said, "Jim, I ain't no rancher. There's several men buried on this ranch that came a long way jist t' die here. I ain't plannin' on bein' among 'em."

"What's yer plans then?" Jim asked.

"Well, I'll tell ya, lettin' ole Mason git the drop on me out there sorta makes me wonder... I might be gittin' a little past my prime... lot's o' things I ain't done yet that I'd like t' do."

Jim poured them another cup of coffee and said, "There's a couple o' things I ain't told ya."

"An' what would they be?" Tuck inquired.

"Well, I never told ya how Becky come t' have that rifle... she snuck it from alongside my Winchester while I was asleep. An' ole Vogel was already through the door an' I never heard a thing til she shot 'im. Ha! you talk about bein' past yer prime."

Tuck cocked his head to one side, eyed Jim critically, and said, "Sneaked up on you? Well you prob'ly thought Becky was gonna git under the blankets with ya an' when she didn't you was too damn proud t' say anything."

"No, seriously, I never heard a thing," Jim confessed with a laugh.

"Yeah, well what else ain't ya told me?"

Jim's face broke into an enormous grin. He rubbed his hands together with relish and said, "Follow me."

He led Tuck upstairs to the closet in the bedroom that had belonged to Klaus Vogel. There on the floor was a large strong box. Jim opened the lid of the chest to reveal its contents. The box was over half full of gold and silver coins.

"For the love of…?" Tuck exclaimed.

"She only took what she could carry. I told her t' take the box. She said that strongbox might tempt ole Pete more than he could stand. Said she had more than enough packed with her t' deposit in the bank at Cheyenne an' more than that in Kentucky. Said fer me an' you t' keep it... she figgered we earned it. See that note there? She sealed it with candle wax and told me it wuz fer you when ya woke up."

The note was lying on top of the cash. Tuck picked it up and broke its seal. A small object fell from inside the note on to the floor. Tuck reached down and picked it up. It was a small arrowhead with a hole drilled in the top. Tuck read the note silently then handed it to Jim.

"Sir Knight:

You kept the promise that you made to me. I'm returning your token of earnest. The fair maiden you sought no longer exists. You conquered the castle. Keep its treasure.

I'm sorry I disappointed you so.
Becky"

The two men talked long into the night. In the morning they walked together in the brisk outdoor air. The sun was barely up and it was cold. Daylight hours were growing increasingly short. Both men shivered as they sipped from the steaming cups they carried.

"Well, what's yer pleasure?" Tuck asked Jim.

"I'm like you. I always wanted t' see what's out west o' here," Jim replied.

"I don't see no need t' stay here do you?"

In response to Tuck's question Jim stepped through the rails of the corral to begin cutting their horses out from the rest.

"Don't fergit t' cut out Cline's mare, I gotta take 'er back t' Cheyenne," Tuck called after him.

After cutting out their own horses Jim turned the others loose to run free. He and Tuck had decided it was a better choice than trying to sell branded horses they couldn't prove they owned.

With all of their belongings packed, only one chore remained prior to leaving. They took all of the sacks they could find and divided the money in the chest among the sacks. They stowed the sacks in their saddlebags and on the packhorses.

When they were at last mounted and ready to leave, Jim turned around for one last look at the house. "Yessir, we'll spend the winter with nice warm gals an' good sippin' whiskey in Cheyenne. Lordy it'd be dull out here. Then when spring comes, we'll be on our way t' Oregon."

Tuck looked at Jim and asked, "Did ya ever think about goin' to church?"

Jim gave him an incredulous look and said, "No, why do you ask?"

"Oh, just wonderin'" was Tuck's reply.

The buckskin was pawing and tossing his head, informing Tuck that he was anxious to go. Tuck patted the horse's neck and said, "Yeah, me too." Then he felt for the small object hanging from a string around his own neck, just to make sure the little treasure was still there. He said to Jim, "It's gonna be a long winter in one of them towns, and you know I hate towns."

Jim raised his eyebrows in mock disbelief and said, "Now Tuck, there's towns, an' then there's towns. In Cheyenne them girls 'r lonely fer me."

Jim spurred Whiskey into action and Tuck's impatient buckskin bolted after her. They were off, trailing the three packhorses.

Upstairs in the house, lying on the bottom of the empty strongbox was Becky's note and another note lying beside it that read:

Neither do I condemn thee.

Tuck

ABOUT THE AUTHOR

Gerald (Jerry) Terrebrood is a 22 year veteran of the U.S. Navy retiring with the rank of LT in 1980. He earned a BA from Central Bible College in 1986, an MA from Assemblies of God Theological Seminary in 1987 and a PhD from Newburgh Theological Seminary in 2012. He pastored three churches, was the Academic Dean at 2 colleges, and the President of two colleges. He retired in February 2006.